TRACKING BACKWARD

TRACKING BACKWARD

To Val,
With appreciation for
all your help, as well
as fond thoughts and
best regards.
Alice Zogg
Oct. 28, 2005

By Alice Zogg

Aventine Press

This book is a work of fiction.

Published by Aventine Press
1023 4th Ave #204
San Diego CA, 92101
www.aventinepress.com

ISBN: 1-59330-309-2

Library of Congress Control Number: 2005933686
Library of Congress Cataloging-in-Publication Data
Tracking Backward/Alice Zogg
Printed in the United States of America

This one's for you, Wilfried

CREDITS

Thanks are in order to Tim McCarron for sharing some of his knowledge about airplanes and aviation. Credit is due to my friend, Karen Carter, for her advice on how to grow and care for orchids. Anthony Thyssen graciously gave his permission to let me use excerpts from his website on building a kite. Thank you, Mr. Thyssen. My friend, Pat Yankosky, used her artistic talents and designed the book cover. Great job, Pat! Valoise Douglas helped make this book a better read with her invaluable editing suggestions. Last but not least, I thank my daughter, Franziska, for her tireless effort of proofreading another of my works.

CAST OF CHARACTERS:

R. A. Huber	Private detective and narrator of this story
Peter Huber	R. A. Huber's husband; an amateur writer
Scott Lamont	Huber's thirteen-year-old client
Steven Lamont	Scott's deceased father
Claire Lamont	Scott's deceased mother
Michelle Lamont	Scott's sister; a college student majoring in philosophy
Suzanne Prescott	Scott's aunt; a real estate agent
Keith Prescott	Suzanne's husband; a mechanical engineer
Nicki Prescott	Scott's cousin; a college sophomore
Vicki Prescott	Scott's cousin; a college freshman
Maryanne Sosna	Scott's aunt; takes her volunteer jobs seriously
Luke Sosna	Maryanne's spouse; a politician
Chris Sosna	Scott's cousin; a high school student
Thomas Teleford	Present owner of Lamont & Associates
Teresa Cesar	Former housekeeper of the Lamont household

Rachael Moreley	Personal secretary of the late Steven Lamont
Shelby	An elementary schoolteacher
James Bradley	Retired accountant of Lamont & Associates
Bill Mc Naught	Airplane mechanic at Truckee Tahoe Airport
Robert Perdue	Owns a roofing business in Reno
Sergeant John Wolf	South Pasadena Homicide detective

Chapter 1

The door to my office was pushed partially open, and a mop of unruly brown hair atop a pair of inquisitive gray eyes appeared.

I said, "Can I help you?"

Leaving the door open behind him, the boy took a few tentative steps towards my desk and said, "I'm looking for the detective."

"That would be me," I stated.

"Oh."

I was clearly not the person he had expected to find, and for a moment it looked like he was going to turn around and leave, but he changed his mind and announced, "I want to hire you. How much do you charge?"

"That depends on what is involved." Then I said, "Please close the door and have a seat."

As he seated himself across the desk from me in the client chair, I extended my hand, saying, "I'm R.A. Huber, and what's your name?"

"Scott Lamont," he replied.

"How old are you, Scott?"

"Thirteen."

"Do your parents know that you are here?"

"My parents are dead."

"Oh, I'm very sorry," I commented.

"I think they were murdered, and I want you to find out who killed them."

I thought, leave it to a child to come straight to the point!

Aloud, I said, "With whom do you live?"

He answered, "I live with Keith and Suzanne Prescott. Suzanne is my aunt and guardian."

Looking at his backpack, I asked, "I take it you came here straight from school?"

"Yeah, I took the bus."

"How did you learn of my detective agency?"

"I found you in the Pasadena yellow pages under 'Investigators.'"

During the entire time we had been talking, the boy had kept his eyes on my chessboard with the set-up chessmen at the far end of the desk.

He suddenly burst out, "Can we play a game?"

"Maybe later. I first want to hear your story." And I added, "When did your parents pass away?"

He replied, "Four years ago."

Surprised, I said, "Oh, that long ago. So you were nine at the time."

"Yes."

"How did they die?"

"My father's plane crashed. I believed it was an accident, but now I think it was murder."

He took a piece of paper from his backpack and handed it to me. I studied it at length. It looked like a draft of a letter, which apparently had not been finished. It was obviously a rough draft, words having been crossed out and sentences started over. It was dated March 1, four years earlier, and it read:

"Dearest Shelby,

As you know, I don't take my cell phone or laptop with me to Tahoe and I don't want to use the house phone to call you. By the time you get this letter, I'll be in L.A. I'm flying down tomorrow morning. I found out (This was crossed out) Something extremely disturbing has come to my attention, and I have to cut my stay up here short.

Things have happened (This was crossed out) I need to investigate the matter further and get proof. It might make a difference in our relationship. I'll explain when I see you in person, my love."

The draft broke off at that point.

Handing the paper back to him, I said, "Looks like a rough draft of a letter written four years ago. Do you know who wrote it?"

"My dad, of course."

"You recognize your father's handwriting?"

"No, I don't know his handwriting, but he must have written it. I found it at our house up at Tahoe. He wrote it the day before he was killed."

I asked, "Who is Shelby?"

"I don't know," he shrugged.

I pointed at the piece of paper and said, "You understand what this implies?"

He nodded, "Yes, Dad had a girlfriend. But that's not important. Don't you see what that letter means! He was going to find proof in Los Angeles, but somebody did something to his plane so it crashed and he couldn't get there."

I said, "Proof of what? Scott, you've got to understand that we have no idea what this draft of a possible letter written to someone named Shelby refers to."

"That's why I want to hire you. To find out."

I stated, "Don't you think it is strange that four years after this draft was written, you found it laying around at your Tahoe residence?"

"It wasn't laying around. It was hidden, and I found it."

Then I asked, "How many other people were on that aircraft?"

He replied, "Just my dad and mom. It was only a little two-seater plane."

"Where did the plane crash?"

"Soon after take-off near Lake Tahoe North Shore."

I looked at him pensively for a while and then stated, "All right, Scott. You had better tell me everything you know. Start by enlightening me about your house at Tahoe."

He stared at me and said, "It's just a house. You mean you want me to tell you about the rooms and furniture and stuff?"

I smiled and said, "No. What I mean is, tell me what you do up there, how often you go there, and with whom."

"Oh, I see. Sometimes we go there in summer, but we always go for skiing and snowboarding every year, the last week of February and the first week of March."

"It's March 11 today, so you must have just come back." And I added, "What do you mean by 'we?'"

"Family and relatives. Sometimes friends come up too."

"I'd like to form an accurate picture, so be more specific, please."

"Okay. When my mom and dad were alive, it was them, my sister Michelle, myself, plus everyone else. Now it's mostly Aunt Suzanne, Uncle Keith, my cousins Nicki and Vicki, my sister and myself. Then there's my Aunt Maryanne, Uncle Luke and their son Chris. Those are the regulars, but sometimes other friends and families will come up too."

I said, "It must be a big house to accommodate all these people."

"Oh, every family has their own house. My parents, which I guess belongs to my sister and me now, the Prescotts and the Sosnas."

Then I asked, "How old is your sister?"

"She is 21 and a junior in college."

"Is it fun to have a sister so much older than you?"

His eyes lit up as he said, "Michelle is the greatest! I wish I could be with her more often."

I said, "Now, tell me how exactly it came about that you found this draft of a letter." And I added, "I assume you found it while on your recent ski vacation at Lake Tahoe?"

"Yes," he said. "I had the flu and couldn't go out snowboarding for three days. I was home alone and it got boring. You can't play computer games all day. Anyhow, my dad had this antique desk and it is still there. I read someplace that some of these desks have secret compartments. I opened all the drawers and fiddled around. I was just going to give up, and gave it a last tap, when part of one side of a drawer caved in and exposed a small hidden compartment. That's where I found the piece of paper."

"I see."

He continued, "I kept reading and re-reading the note. I am sure my parents were murdered. It can't be a coincidence that Dad was on his way to find out about some crime and accidentally crashed his plane."

"I can understand that you think that way, but we don't know if it was a question of a crime being committed. The letter might have referred to something minor."

He looked at me pleadingly and said, "Please find out for me."

Pointing at the note, I asked, "Did you show or tell about this to anyone?"

"No."

"Not even your sister?"

"I wanted to tell Michelle, but we were never alone. She had some friends with her up at Tahoe. Now I'm kind of glad I didn't. She probably would've told me to forget about it and leave it alone."

"That would have been good advice," I remarked.

Clearly disappointed, he said, "So you won't help me?"

"Scott, do you realize that if I took this job on, and it turns out that your suspicion is correct, I might uncover things that would be painful for you?"

He thought about this for a moment, then replied, "I think I know what you mean. The murderer might not be a stranger."

"Exactly."

He looked me in the eye and stated, "I still want to know what happened."

After a long pause, I said, "All right. I'll look into the matter for you. Whether I'll be successful with this investigation after four years have passed is doubtful. But I'll try."

"Cool!"

He reached into his backpack, took some cash out of an envelope and counted out the bills, one by one. There was an assortment of twenties, tens and singles. The total amount came to $496.00.

Handing me the money, he said, "I hope this is enough for a down payment."

I asked, "Where did you get this money?"

"I've been saving my allowance for a new mountain bike, but the bike will have to wait."

"You must have been saving for a long time?"

"Almost a year. I get $50.00 a month. I spent some of it, though." And then he said, "I have money in the bank, but it's in a trust account. I can't withdraw any of it without my guardian's signature until I'm eighteen. Michelle got her inheritance when she was eighteen. So I'm planning to borrow some from her to pay you the rest."

I stated, "I tell you what. I'll take one month's worth of your allowance as a down payment. And let's not worry about the rest for the time being."

I pocketed $50.00, replaced the remainder of his money in the envelope, and handed it back.

Then I said, "Okay, Scott. I need lots more information from you. What were your parents' names and professions?"

He replied, "Steven and Claire Lamont. My dad was a broker. I don't remember what my mom did."

"Do you remember the name of the brokerage firm your father worked for?"

"Lamont & Associates."

"Oh, he owned his own business. Does it still exist?"

"Yes. His partner, Thomas Teleford, owns it now."

Then I asked, "You told me that you live with your aunt and uncle. Where is that?"

"In San Remos."

"I believe that's a small town in the general Arcadia area?"

"Yes, it's not far from here," he replied.

"Did you live in the same town with your parents when they were alive?"

"No. We lived in Santa Lucia then."

"Oh yes, I know Santa Lucia."

I paused, thinking how best to word the next question. Then I inquired, "This might be hard for you to remember, since you were only nine at the time, but did your household consist of other people besides your parents, your sister and yourself?"

He answered, "I was nine, not a baby!" Then he softened a bit, "We had Tesa, the housekeeper. Her name was actually Teresa, but when I was little, I couldn't pronounce it, so I always called her Tesa."

I handed him a yellow legal pad and pen, saying, "Please put down your sister's name, address and telephone number, as well as the same information of your other relatives."

He complied and listed Michelle Lamont, Keith and Suzanne Prescott, and their addresses and phone numbers.

When he got to Luke and Maryanne Sosna, he paused and said, "My Aunt Maryanne and Uncle Luke live near Washington, D.C. I don't know their address and phone number by heart."

"That's okay. You can give it to me later." And I added, "Do you have a last name for Teresa, by any chance?"

"No."

"No matter," I said, "I can probably get information about her from someone else."

Scott gave me a disarming smile and said, "If you find Tesa, I want to see her again too. I liked her. She used to sing to me."

Then I held out my hand "Let me borrow the note."

"Sure, I know it by heart."

I looked at my watch, then at the boy, and said, "I think that wraps it up for now. It's ten past four. Your aunt might worry about you by now."

"I doubt it. She's probably still working."

"Who would miss you, then?"

He grinned and said, "My soccer coach. I was supposed to go to practice right after school."

"Are you going to be in trouble?"

"Probably, but I don't care. Hiring you is more important."

I said, "All right, Scott. How about that game of chess I promised you earlier?"

His eyes opened wide, and he exclaimed, "Cool!"

Soon it became apparent that Scott was a skillful player. As the chess match progressed, I was amazed at the boy's prowess. I pride myself on showing command of the game, but I was checkmated in less than 40 moves!

I declared, "Young man! You certainly are a master at this!"

He grinned from ear to ear.

Then I said, "Now, how about if I give you a ride home?"

"Thanks!" he replied, still smiling, as we got up and made our way to the parking lot.

Chapter 2

Following dinner that Thursday, March 11, my husband, Peter, said, "You came home rather late today. Did you drum up some new sleuthing business?"

"Yes, but I might make it a pro bono case," I said.

"Oh?"

"I have a new client. A boy of thirteen, to be exact."

And I proceeded to tell him all about it. Having finished the story, I handed him the draft letter.

Peter read the note carefully, and then stated, "This is a vague draft. Obviously the writer did not finish it, and of course it's not signed. As far as I can see, nothing in it indicates a crime had been committed. It suggests to me that the writer had an affair with someone named Shelby and couldn't wait to tell her about some discovery or other."

Then he added, "How can the boy, I think you said Scott is his name, even be sure that his father had written this note?"

"It pretty much stands to reason that Scott's father was the writer of this draft. The boy found it in the late Mr. Lamont's desk at his residence at Tahoe. The note was dated March 1 of that year, and, in it is stated that the writer was going to fly to the L.A. area the next day, which Scott's dad obviously tried to do when his plane crashed."

Peter said, "Okay. So we take it as fact that the draft was written by Mr. Lamont, but come now, Regula, you can't seriously consider this piece of paper any evidence that the plane had been sabotaged. In my opinion, this assumption was made by Scott's romantic notion."

"There is nothing romantic about having one's parents murdered," I remarked.

He countered, "It might be, to a boy of thirteen."

"Well," I said, "This woman of sixty or so thinks there was clearly an indication of urgency on the part of Scott's father. He dropped everything, cut his ski vacation short, and flew home to investigate!"

"Yes, I'll grant you that. But I'm still surprised that you agreed to look into this. I'm sure you've given some thought to how hard it'll be to investigate, four years later."

"My task won't be easy, I know."

Then he said, "Do you have a plan?"

I replied, "I'll have to find a way to get the plane crash info. There is always an investigation after an accident, but I have no idea who to contact. And if I should happen to find the correct agency, it's questionable whether they'll be willing to dig up the report four years later."

Peter suggested, "I would presume you'll find the NTSB on the Web."

"What is NTSB?"

"National Transportation Safety Board."

"And they're the ones that handle air crash accidents?"

"Yes, among other things," he said.

I exclaimed, "You are a fountain of knowledge, Peter! Thanks!"

Then he asked, "What else is on your agenda?"

"I'll talk to Scott's relatives. I hope they all have good memories. I'm going to tackle Michelle, the sister, first."

"What sort of a boy is Scott?"

"Intelligent and mature for his age, and independent, I think."

With a twinkle in his eye, my husband asked, "So if

you're taking this job on pro bono, out of the goodness of your heart to help the boy out, why did you take his fifty bucks?"

Smiling, I replied, "I didn't want to offend him."

"Come again?"

"Scott struck me as a business-minded kid. His first question to me was, 'How much do you charge?' If I would have refused a down payment, he'd have thought me incompetent."

"So how come you didn't take all the money he offered?"

"I didn't want him to have to save his allowance for another year before he can buy his mountain bike."

Peter commented, "You're a softy, Regula! He sounds like a rich kid to me. I'm sure his aunt can afford to buy him a bike."

"Sure, but I had the feeling he likes to be independent and make his own purchases."

Then I laughed and said, "I found Scott to be a remarkable boy, in many ways. He beat me at chess!"

Peter blurted, "Aha! Now I know why you accepted the case. You want a rematch!"

Chapter 3

Igot comfortable in the computer room that evening and did my research. I found the National Transportation Safety Board site and clicked on the aviation category. To my amazement I discovered a listing of accidents dating back from 1962 all the way to the present. I clicked on March four years earlier.

There were columns with the following headings: Date of accident, location, aircraft type, registration number, severity, and type of carrier. To the far left, there was also a column with the word *final* underlined and a date next to it. I presumed this was when the investigation was concluded. I checked through the listing.

Then I shouted, "Bingo!"

Peter called out from the living room, "Are you talking to yourself, Regula?"

"Come here and look at this," I said.

I showed him my find. Date: March 2 four years earlier. Location: Sierra Nevada Mountains, near Lake Tahoe, California. Aircraft type: Cessna 152. Severity: two fatalities. Type of carrier: General Aviation.

"Yep! You found it," he said.

I commented, "How did we ever manage before we had the Internet?"

Then I clicked on the word *final* with the date January 14 of the year after the crash next to it, and I got the following report:

"According to the flight plan filed, the Cessna 152 took off from Truckee airport at 9:10 a.m. and was headed for the Van Nuys airport. Estimated flight time: three hours.

No radio contact was made. There were no witnesses to the crash. The pilot did not close his arrival time in the air near his destination. When the aircraft failed to arrive at Van Nuys airport as scheduled, an alert was put out for the Cessna 152 at 12:45 p.m. and a search flight was sent out. The plane was sighted at 1:10 p.m. and located by the ground search and rescue team at 2:25 p.m.

"Evidently, the plane lost power soon after take-off, stalled, crashed into a tree in the Sierra Nevada Mountains, and then caught fire. Probable cause: inconclusive. Weather was not a factor. It was sunny and clear. Could have been caused by mechanical failure or pilot error. Another possibility could have been that the pilot was disabled due to sudden illness, such as stroke or heart attack. Service records at Truckee airport showed that engine oil was changed on February 27. Nothing out of the ordinary was noticed during servicing."

My initial excitement of finding the report soon came to a halt. I printed the page out and then read it once more.

Peter, sensing my disappointment, said, "Well, what did you expect?"

I replied, "I don't know what I had in mind." And I added, "I guess I'm just frustrated that there's nothing in the report I can sink my teeth into."

He stated, "Don't forget, this was an accident inquiry, not a murder investigation. The crash might prove to be nothing more than a devastating act of fate."

Chapter 4

On the way to my office in Pasadena the following day, leaving my hometown, Merida, and entering the 210 East freeway, I suddenly had a brainstorm: Santa Lucia! Of course!

The minute I arrived at my desk, I looked up the number and dialed Sergeant John Wolf's extension at South Pasadena Homicide.

"Hello, Sergeant Wolf? R.A. Huber here."

"Well, hi there, R.A. Huber! Last I heard you were living it up on Catalina Island!"

I could picture Wolf clearly in my mind. The bushy brows over alert brown eyes and the broad, muscular build. What I remembered most were his oversized hands.

I laughed and said, "That wouldn't be my choice of words!" And I added, "Since you mention my case in Avalon, thank you for clearing my name with Detective Ron Barker."

"Barker's bark is worse than his bite! Ha ha!" He laughed at his own joke. Then he said, "So what's up?"

"I have a favor to ask. I wonder if you can give me some information?"

"I didn't think this was a social call. So shoot."

I asked, "Is Santa Lucia still your jurisdiction?"

"Sure," he replied.

"I am looking into a private plane accident that happened four years ago. The plane crashed near North Shore Lake Tahoe, but the two fatality victims were residents of Santa Lucia."

"I'm in homicide. Plane crash accidents have nothing to do with our department."

"Oh, I know. But it might turn out to be murder."

The sergeant said, "This happened four years ago, you said?"

"Yes."

"Tell me the story, R.A. Huber."

I proceeded to tell him what I had learned from Scott Lamont, without mentioning any names.

Then he said, "You've got little to go on. There is no way an official homicide investigation can be launched on such skimpy information."

I replied, "I know, Sergeant. I'm planning to question the persons concerned, and hopefully will come up with more evidence."

"I see."

I continued, "I checked the National Transportation Safety Board's website and found the plane crash in question."

"What were their findings?"

I extracted the printout from my purse and then read the entire NTSB report to the sergeant.

When I finished, he said, "Inconclusive. Mechanical failure or pilot error; sounds like it was undetermined what exactly caused the crash."

I asked, "If I find evidence of possible foul play, would the NTSB reopen their investigation?"

He replied, "Possibly, but you would need substantial evidence." And he added, "Their final findings came to a conclusion the following January, so that's over three years ago. I doubt very much that they could add anything crucial to their report, even if willing to reopen the case. The scent is cold by now, Mrs. Huber!"

"Yes, I'm afraid so."

I paused and then asked, "If there was sufficient evidence to justify a murder investigation, in whose jurisdiction would the case be?"

Sergeant Wolf said, "You mentioned the two victims were residents of Santa Lucia, but the question of jurisdiction depends on a lot of factors, such as where the crime was committed, whether the perpetrator was responsible for other crimes at different locations, et cetera. In this case, and after such a time lapse, it might be hard to determine."

"I'd just like to get an idea of what agency to contact, once further along with the case."

He laughed and said, "I can tell there is no doubt in your mind that there will be a case!" And he added, "First gather the evidence, then call me, and I'll send you to the proper law enforcement agency."

On that note, we ended the call.

I spent a good part of that Friday scheduling appointments. None of the people I contacted were thrilled to meet with me, which was understandable. Michelle Lamont agreed to see me at her apartment located near the UCLA campus the next day, Saturday. Scott had provided me with Suzanne Prescott's work and home phone numbers. I dialed her business number, and it turned out to be a real estate company. Mrs. Prescott didn't want to meet with me at work. Her Saturday was taken up with showing houses to clients, so she asked me to come to her residence in San Remos on Sunday.

I found Lamont & Associates listed in the Los Angeles phone book. I asked for Mr. Thomas Teleford. At first it looked like I wasn't going to get past his secretary. I was persistent, however. I stated it was of the utmost importance that I talk to Mr. Teleford regarding a private matter concerning the Lamont family. When I finally got him on the line and explained the business at hand, he was not pleased. Nonetheless, our conversation ended with his promise that he could give me half an hour's time on Monday at 10:00 a.m.

Chapter 5

Not familiar with the area, I surprised myself by finding Michelle Lamont's street and address right away, without having to make any U-turns or detours. I was fifteen minutes early for my appointment so I strolled around the grounds. The apartment complex was comprised of six separate two-story buildings constructed around a center area, which sported a swimming pool, recreation room, gym and laundry room. Judging by the young people hanging around, I presumed the tenants were mostly college students. The six apartment structures were marked with letters ranging from A to F. Each building housed eight apartments.

I had just found building D, had mounted the stairs to apartment number 7, and had placed my finger on the doorbell, when I heard footsteps, and someone behind me said, "Mrs. Huber?"

I turned around. I was looking at a young woman who was carrying a laundry basket full of clothes, neatly folded and stacked. She was about my height of 5'6" and slender. Her brown, wavy hair was kept in a short style. The most remarkable feature about her was her eyes. They were penetrating, bright, and green.

I said, "Yes, I am she. And you are Ms Lamont?"

"Call me Michelle." Then she ushered me inside, and pointing straight ahead, she said, "Have a seat in the living room. I'll just put the laundry away." And she added, "Want something to drink?"

"A glass of water would be great. Thanks!"

The living room was cozy and comfortable. The furniture was comprised of pieces from different periods, but somehow it all blended together well. I was engrossed in what I saw hanging on the walls. Drawings and framed quotes of ancient Greek philosophers - -including Socrates, Aristotle, Archimedes, Homer and some I had never heard of - -adorned those walls.

I was still absorbed in the pictures and quotes when Michelle came into the room carrying my glass of water and a can of Coke for her.

I stated, "You keep good company!"

She agreed, "Yeah, they make sure I stay humble!"

Pointing at the walls, I said, "Is this just a hobby of yours, or does it involve your studies?"

"My major is philosophy. I find the subject fascinating." Then, coming straight to the point, she asked, "What is this business about my parents' plane crash? There was an investigation of the accident at the time, so why do it again four years later?"

"There is a possibility that it was not an accident. The plane might have been tampered with."

She raised her eyebrows. Then she said, "That's ridiculous. Who would have wanted to harm my parents?"

"It's my task to find out," I said.

"Who hired you?"

"Your brother."

She looked at me incredulously and said, "Scott? But he was a little kid at the time!"

I reached into my purse, took out the draft, and handing it to her, I said, "Scott found this in your father's desk at Lake Tahoe a few days ago."

She read the note carefully and then remarked, "Poor Scott. He idolized Dad. Finding out Dad had a mistress must have shocked him."

I stated, "Scott didn't seem troubled by that implication in the note. He put all his emphasis on the other matter stated in the draft."

Michelle declared, "By the time Scott talked to you, he must've had ample time to get used to the idea."

I inquired, "The fact that your father might have kept a mistress does not shock you?"

She smiled sadly and replied, "I was seventeen at the time, and I loved my parents. Maybe it would have shocked me then. But I'm a grown woman now, and I understand that one's parents are only human."

"Spoken like a true philosopher!" Then I asked, "Do you know who Shelby is?"

"No, I have no clue."

Then, amused, it seemed, she said, "So Scott hired you." And she exclaimed, "Of course, that's what he wanted to borrow the money for! The day after we came back from Tahoe he called and asked to borrow a thousand dollars."

"Really?"

"When I wanted to know what he needed the money for, he said, 'Never mind, then,' and hung up. I was going to phone him back later to find out why he would suddenly need that kind of money, but I got busy studying and forgot to make the call. I've been busy trying to catch up after a week of missing school."

I said, "I thought it was a two-week ski trip?"

"Oh, it was for everyone else, but I couldn't justify being absent from my classes that long and just went for the last week."

"I see."

Then she commented, "I'm surprised he got the money from Aunt Suzanne. I'm sure he didn't let her know what he needed it for, since he wasn't willing to tell me."

I smiled and said, "He was more resourceful than that. He made a down payment with his hard-earned allowance money!"

"The little stinker!" she said laughingly.

Then she grabbed the draft letter once more and reread it. Handing it back, she said, "There is nothing precise in this note. The statement, 'I need to further investigate the matter and get proof,' could refer to anything in God's creation."

"Yes, I know. I was hoping you could give me a rough idea," I said.

"I really don't know."

Then I asked, "Would your father have cut his ski vacation short for any trivial reason?"

She stated, "Absolutely not. Those two weeks at Tahoe North Shore every year were his way of relaxing and being with the family. He never took work along, and people at his office were not supposed to call him up there, unless it was an emergency."

"Do you know when, exactly, your dad decided to fly to Los Angeles? The note was obviously written the day before the plane crash. It might help to know with whom your father had spent that last day and evening."

She said, "I was with Dad that last day. He did not mention his plan to fly down."

After a pause, I said, "This might be painful for you, but please tell me everything you remember about that day."

"Oh, I remember it clearly. I'm not a nostalgic person as a rule, but after the accident I thought about those last hours spent with my dad."

She started her narrative, "It was a picture-perfect day for skiing, sunny and four inches of fresh powder, since it had snowed the night before. A whole group of us started the day by skiing and snowboarding together - -"

I broke in, "Who was in the group?"

"Dad, Mom, Scott, Aunt Suzanne, Uncle Keith, my cousins Nicki and Vicki, Uncle Luke, my cousin Chris and me."

"Sorry I interrupted."

"As I said, the conditions were perfect and we had a ball skiing and boarding together all morning at Northstar. We all sat around a big table for lunch at the lodge. Then we broke up for the afternoon. Chris and Scott went off with their snowboards by themselves. Mom and Aunt Suzanne quit skiing for the day and went to the Sosna's house to help Aunt Maryanne with some fund-raiser she was organizing. Uncle Keith and Uncle Luke went off together. Nicki and Vicki took the opportunity and sneaked away by themselves as well. They were rather boy-crazy in those days, and welcomed any chance to get away from adult supervision."

Michelle smiled in remembrance as she continued, "Then Dad winked at me and said, 'Just you and me, babe! Let's go find a bunch of black diamond runs and do some real funky skiing!' We had an awesome time together for the rest of the day. Everyone in the family is a good skier, but Dad was absolutely tops."

She came to a halt and said, "There was certainly nothing sinister in my dad's last day."

I said, "I'm glad you have such a perfect day to remember him by."

Then I questioned, "What about in the evening? Do you remember anyone that came to visit, or anyone he had a private talk with?"

She thought about this and then stated, "I know Dad was angry at someone that evening. I remember I went up to my room after dinner to do homework."

"You took homework with you on your vacation?"

"Oh yes. All us kids had to, otherwise the teachers wouldn't have let us miss school. We had to study and make up what we missed. A certain amount of money is withheld from the school for each day a student is absent for any reason other than illness. Nothing was ever said about it, but I had a sneaky feeling that our families made up the amounts to the schools."

I said, "Sorry for interrupting again. You were saying you had gone to your room to do homework."

"Yes. My room was right above the den, and I heard Dad yell at somebody."

"Do you know whom he was shouting at?"

"No, but I was surprised. I had never heard my dad raise his voice to anyone. He usually got his point across quietly and precisely."

I asked, "Did you hear the other person respond?"

She replied, "No. Frankly, it disturbed me to hear Dad's angry voice, so I turned my music up and tuned it out."

"Did you get the feeling that he was talking to someone in the room with him, or did you think he was on the phone?"

"I don't know."

I pressed further, "Do you remember the words your dad shouted?"

After a pause, Michelle said, "I think it was something like, 'You lousy bit of shit! How long has this been going on?' But I can't be sure. I tried to forget it, especially after what happened the following day."

"Yes. I can understand that," I said.

Then I asked, "Your cousins, Nicki and Vicki, are they twins?"

"No, but less than a year apart in age," she replied.

"How old were they at the time?"

"Fifteen and sixteen."

"And you were seventeen," I said. "Were you boy-crazy as well?"

She laughed and said, "Boys my age bored me. As a matter of fact, they still do."

"Is there an older man in your life?"

With a twinkle in her bright, green eyes, she stated, "Yes. He's not ancient, though. He just turned thirty."

Then I asked, "Do you know why your mother joined your father on that flight?"

She reflected, and then said, "I can't remember exactly. I think there was some kind of a medical reason, and Mom had to go home to see a doctor. Might have been an earache or something; I can't recall."

"I see." And I added, "Scott couldn't remember what your mom's profession was."

"She was a librarian. I'm not surprised that Scott doesn't remember. He was little at the time, and Mom and Dad rarely talked shop, neither about Dad's business nor about Mom's work."

After a lengthy pause, I said, "I have one more question and then I won't intrude on you any longer. Scott mentioned a housekeeper, Teresa, whom he called Tesa."

"What's the question?"

"Do you happen to know her last name?"

"It was Valdez, but now she's married to Julius Cesar."

I remarked, "Mr. Cesar's parents must have had a sense of humor!"

She stared and then said, "Oh, that's funny. I never thought of it before."

I asked further, "By any chance, do you have Teresa Cesar's address?"

Michelle stated, "You're thorough, Mrs. Huber! I do keep in touch with Teresa. Aunt Suzanne, my guardian until I was eighteen, agreed to let me stay in our house in Santa Lucia, so I didn't have to change schools in my last year of high school. I lived there by myself and Teresa stayed with me until I started college. Her cheerful personality helped me a lot during those first few months after my parents' death."

She went over to a small desk, took out a pen and notepaper, and wrote down Teresa Cesar's address and phone number. Then she handed me the piece of paper and said, "Tell her I sent you. Teresa was always protective of our family and might not talk to you otherwise."

I got up to leave and said, "Thank you very much. I really appreciate that you were so open with me today."

As Michelle walked me to the door, she shook her head and remarked, "I wish Scott would've left it alone. He might get hurt if you succeed in your investigation."

"I think he's aware of that, but he wants to know."

I left her standing at her apartment's threshold, a meditative look on her face.

Chapter 6

On Sunday afternoon I drove to the small town of San Remos. Finding the Prescott residence was easy. I had paid attention when dropping Scott off on the previous Thursday. The raised ranch style home situated at the end of a *cul-de-sac* boasted an attached double garage, a low-pitched gabled roof, and large windows with green shutters.

The woman who invited me in was obviously the lady of the house. She was petite, a little on the chubby side, a redhead in her early forties, and extremely animated. I followed her into a spacious living room which was furnished early American style. I declined her offer of a beverage, and we seated ourselves on upholstered chairs, facing one another across the coffee table.

Suzanne Prescott wasted no time and got straight to the subject. "You told me on the phone that Scott found a letter. Please show it to me."

"It's only a draft," I said, and handed it over.

After reading it, she shook her head saying, "I don't understand why Scott didn't come to me with this. Frankly, I'm offended that he secretly went off by himself to hire an investigator."

I asked, "Had he confided in you, what would your advice have been?"

She chuckled and admitted, "There's my answer, I guess! I would've told him to forget about it." Then she got serious and stated, "I don't see what good this investigation can possibly do the boy, but since I can't stop it, I'll cooperate."

"I appreciate that."

She continued, "Scott is at a friend's house. I thought it was best if he wasn't here during our talk. My husband is running errands but should be back soon. I doubt he'll be able to tell you more than I can, though."

Then she said, "All right, what do you want to know?"

I liked the woman's directness. I asked, "Do you know who Shelby is?"

"Never heard the name."

"Did you ever suspect that your brother had a mistress?"

"No, but the note to this Shelby person seems to indicate that there was one."

"After four years, it is hard to piece things together. I'm trying to get a picture in my mind of all the persons present at Lake Tahoe at the time. I'm sure you can help me with that. Try to remember exactly who was there on that particular trip."

She said, "Let's see. There was the Lamont family. That's my brother Steven, my sister-in-law Claire, Michelle and Scott. Then there was the Sosna family. That would be my brother-in-law Luke, my sister Maryanne and their son Chris. My husband Keith and I were there with our daughters Nicki and Vicki. Let me think now. - - Oh, yes, Thomas Teleford was there that year also."

She came to a stop and said, "I hope I didn't forget anyone."

"Scott informed me of the houses each family owned at Lake Tahoe, but he didn't mention that his father's partner had one."

"Oh, Thomas doesn't own a home up there. We purchased the properties over fifteen years ago. By the time Thomas joined us on our trips, there were no houses up for sale in that area. He always rented a place in the condominium complex a little bit down the road."

"I see." And I asked, "Did Mr. Teleford bring his family along?"

She replied, "Thomas was divorced. He brought his girlfriend, but I can't remember her name at the moment." And she added, "He's remarried now. He came up with his new wife this year."

"Does he have any children?"

She had to think this over and then stated, "He might from his prior marriage, but I really don't know. If he has any, he certainly never brought them to Tahoe."

"I have an appointment to see Mr. Teleford tomorrow. I'll ask him."

I had to think of how to formulate my next words delicately, so it wouldn't sound offensive, and then I asked, "Did the question of adopting Scott after his parents' tragic accident ever come up?" And I quickly added, "I hope you don't think me impertinent to inquire?"

She replied, "I don't mind telling you. There was a will, of course. My brother and sister-in-law stated in their will that I should bring up Michelle and Scott if they both died before the children became adults. I was named as their guardian until they reached the age of eighteen. Michelle was practically an adult, short only by one year.

"Keith and I discussed adopting Scott and couldn't decide what was best. After all, the boy was nine years old and had loved and lived with his parents long enough to form an opinion of who he was. In the end we left it up to Scott to make the decision. He chose not to be adopted."

I commented, "I have the feeling Scott is an independent boy."

"Yes he is, and always was."

"I talked to Michelle yesterday. She told me that you had agreed to let her stay at her parents' residence with the housekeeper, in order to finish her senior high school year in Santa Lucia."

She said, "Indeed I did! Michelle was a mature girl. I never regretted that decision."

Then I asked, "Do you enjoy your job as a real estate agent?"

"Oh, very much so," she replied. "It's exciting to find the perfect homes for my clients."

"What does your husband do?"

"He's a mechanical engineer."

"Are your daughters away at college?"

"Yes. They both attend UC Irvine."

After a pause, I said, "Scott told me that the Sosnas live in Washington, D.C. What are their professions?"

"My brother-in-law is a congressman, and my sister is involved with doing volunteer work."

"I'd appreciate it if you'd let me have their phone number and address. I'm not planning to fly to D.C., but I need to talk to them. It might not be easy for me to contact them, so a word of introduction from you would help a lot."

She laughed. "You're in luck, Mrs. Huber. They had to delay their ski trip this year and are flying to Tahoe either tomorrow or Tuesday for their two-week stay."

"How lucky! Congressman Sosna is probably more approachable on his vacation than he would be in Washington," I said.

At that moment the door opened and I was introduced to Keith Prescott. Mr. Prescott was a man in his forties with a round amiable face, a balding head and he carried a little potbelly.

After we shook hands, he said, "Suzanne told me about you and the reason you're here. Although I admire Scott's spunk, I think he's wasting your time."

"You might be right. The plane crash could prove to be merely an accident, but you can't blame your nephew for wanting to find out the truth."

He shrugged his shoulders and said, "I guess not."

Then I said, "I have already asked your wife and got an answer in the negative. Do you know anyone by the first name of Shelby?"

He thought about it and then replied, "No, I can't think of anyone by that name."

I turned to the lady of the house and stated, "Could I get your daughters' addresses and phone numbers, please? And I would appreciate the Sosnas' number at their Tahoe residence as well."

Suzanne Prescott said, "Our daughters have the same phone number and address. They share an apartment near the UC Irvine campus. I'll give it to you, even though I doubt they can tell you anything about the matter. I can't give you the Sosnas' number; it's unlisted. I'll call my sister and let her know you want to get in touch with them."

"That would be greatly appreciated."

Then I addressed them both, "Do either of you remember why Mrs. Lamont joined her husband on that fatal flight?"

"Yes, I remember," Mrs. Prescott said. "Claire had a horrible toothache. Apparently she had lost a filling at dinner the night before. Anyhow, she called me just before they left that morning. She explained that Steven was flying down to L.A. and she had decided to go with him, since she needed to see her dentist."

I thanked them for their time, tucked the Nicki/Vicki information into my purse, and left the Prescotts to what was left of their Sunday.

Chapter 7

On Monday morning, March 15, driving to my appointment with the present owner of Lamont & Associates, I was rehearsing my questions. Since Mr. Thomas Teleford had made it clear that I would be given half an hour of his time and no more, I planned to be brief, precise, and to the point.

I found a spot in the visitor's parking area in the underground garage of that particular office building. The high rise didn't distinguish itself from any of the others along that city block in the greater Los Angeles area. Lamont & Associates was situated at street level, and it looked like the company had the whole floor to themselves.

I gave the receptionist my name and was told to have a seat. The furniture and décor in the reception area was obviously created to give an image of prosperity. At ten o'clock sharp I was ushered into Thomas Teleford's office. The man got up from behind his desk, extended his hand and said, "Nice to meet you, Mrs. Huber."

I shook his hand firmly and said, "I appreciate your making time for me, Mr. Teleford."

I studied him for a brief moment. What I saw was a man in his forties, tall and solidly built. He had brown eyes, a long face and kept his dark hair cut short. There was something commanding and authoritative about his face.

He briskly said, "So. What, exactly, is this all about?"

I stated, "I was hired by a family member to look into the fatal plane crash of Steven and Claire Lamont."

Somehow I could not bring myself to tell this man that a thirteen-year-old boy had employed me. Consequently I did not mention the draft letter.

He said, "Why?"

"There is new information indicating it might have been foul play," I said.

"Oh?"

Getting no reply from me, he stated, "I imagine this would be difficult to investigate after four years."

"Yes. I have to track backward, so to speak. You might be able to help with this task."

"I doubt it."

I continued, "I understand you were part of the skiing group at Lake Tahoe that year?"

"Yes, I was there."

"Do you have any idea why the late Mr. Lamont suddenly decided to cut his ski vacation short and fly back home?"

"No, I don't. By the way, it could easily have been me that would've been killed in that crash along with Steven, instead of Claire."

Surprised, I asked, "How come?"

"I was going to fly back with Steven, but then Claire apparently had a tooth emergency and needed to see her dentist immediately."

Puzzled, I said, "I don't understand. If Mr. Lamont's flight back to Los Angeles was spontaneous, how could it have been planned that you would fly with him?"

He explained, "I only had time to stay a few days at Lake Tahoe that year. If I remember correctly, everyone else had planned the usual trip of two weeks. I had a commercial plane reservation out of Reno for my flight back to L.A. on the day of Steven's accident. The night before, Steven told me that he was flying down the next

morning and that I could join him. He knew, of course, that
I was scheduled to go back that day. I took his offer and
was going to cancel my reservation with the commercial
airline the following morning. However, he called me
early that morning and told me I could not fly with him
after all, since he had to take Claire. His plane was a little
two-seater Cessna 152."

After a pause, he commented, "It has haunted me ever
since that Claire died in that crash instead of me."

I asked, "The evening before the crash, when you
talked to Mr. Lamont, was that at his house?"

He looked at me impatiently and then said, "No.
Steven called me."

I could tell he thought, what difference does it make?
He obviously did not know I had the loud confrontation
at the house between Lamont and someone in mind when
asking that question.

Then I said, "I take it that you didn't own your own
plane, like Mr. Lamont?"

"I didn't then, but I have one now." And he continued,
"Actually, it was Steven who got me interested in flying. I
had started to take flying instructions a few weeks before
Steven's accident. Then after the crash, I was on the verge
of giving the whole thing up. A few months later I pulled
myself together, continued the flight-training and got my
pilot license about a year later."

I asked, "Is your plane also a Cessna?"

"No, it's a Beechcraft Baron."

"Forgive my ignorance, but is that also a little two-
seater plane?"

"No," he said, "it's a twin engine, six passenger."

Then I inquired, "Did Mr. Lamont have a personal
secretary?"

"Yes."

"Is she still with the company?"

"Since we had no need for her after the accident, I let her go."

"No one I've talked to so far seems to know the reason why Mr. Lamont suddenly cut his vacation short. Maybe he had an appointment, and there might be a chance his secretary would remember with whom he was planning to meet."

Mr. Teleford said, "I doubt it, but you can try." And he pushed his intercom button, saying, "Monique."

A few seconds later, an attractive young woman appeared, smiled at me, then turned to her employer. "Yes, Mr. Teleford?"

"Get Rachael Moreley's address and number from personnel for Mrs. Huber, please."

Monique was out the door again in a flash.

Then I said, "Suzanne Prescott named everyone she remembered in the group of people at Lake Tahoe that year. She mentioned that you had brought along a girlfriend."

Clearly annoyed, he said, "I'm married now. I don't see any reason why you should question a former friend of mine."

I quickly replied, "Oh, I have no intention to talk to her. I am just curious; would she have taken that commercial flight by herself if you had flown with Mr. Lamont?"

He stared. Then he laughed and said, "You are a dangerous woman, R.A. Huber. Anyone with something to hide would have to be careful when talking with you!" Then he said, "My friend happened to live in Northern California, and regardless of how I left Tahoe, she was driving home by herself."

At that moment Monique reappeared and handed me the requested information. I thanked her. She smiled and then vanished.

I turned my attention back to Mr. Teleford and asked, "Were you Steven Lamont's only partner?"

"Yes."

"I'm just curious, but did you ever think of changing the name of the business?"

"The question came up at the time, but I decided against it."

"Why was that?"

He explained, "Although a small brokerage firm, Lamont & Associates was well established and had the reputation of conducting business with integrity. I felt it was best to keep the name." And he added, "Besides, I owed it to Steven's memory."

"I understand." Then I asked, "Do you have any children?"

"I have a grown daughter. She never came up to Tahoe with me. I'd appreciate if you keep her out of this matter."

The way he said this, it was obviously not a request, but rather an order. Then he looked at his watch, and I knew my time was up.

I was already on the drive back to my office when it occurred to me that I had forgotten to ask Mr. Teleford if he knew anyone by the name of Shelby.

Chapter 8

Teresa Cesar and I were to meet in a small neighborhood park in Pasadena that Monday afternoon.

I was there first so I sat down on a bench, amusing myself by watching the traffic of little kids on their bicycles, roller blades and scooters. Some of them wore knee, elbow, and wrist pads, but they all had donned helmets. I was just reflecting on what a cautious, protective society we'd become when a woman walked toward me. She had a graceful gait, and as she came closer, I perceived a full head of dark hair, brown eyes, and a mouth that seemed turned up at the corners in a permanent little smile. I judged her to be in her mid-thirties.

She said, "Mrs. Huber?"

"Yes. And you must be Teresa Cesar," I said.

As she joined me on the bench, she stated, "I'm glad we agreed to meet in the park. It's a beautiful day."

I said, "I appreciate your willingness to talk to me."

"Michelle called me and said I should answer your questions. I wouldn't have talked to you otherwise." And she added, "But I really don't know anything about the plane accident."

"Oh, my questions won't concern the plane crash. I just want to get a general idea about the Lamont household, before and around the time of the tragedy." Then I asked, "Did you ever go along with the family on their trips to Lake Tahoe?"

"Never. They didn't need me up there. They ate most of their meals out, and a cleaning crew took care of everything after they left. I'm glad they didn't take me along on their skiing trips. I don't like cold weather."

"So when the family went up to Tahoe you had a chance of a little free time to yourself?"

"Yes," she replied. "I usually went to my native country to see my mother."

"Which country is that?"

"Panama."

I complimented, "You speak English well. Have you been here long?"

"Fourteen years. And with a big grin, she added, "I became a citizen of the United States two years ago!"

"We have something in common. I wasn't born here either and became a citizen about thirty years ago."

She inquired, "Are you from Germany?"

"No, Switzerland."

She commented, "So you have dual citizenship?"

"Yes," I replied, amazed at her knowledge.

Then I felt it was time to come to the point and asked, "How long had you been employed by the Lamont family?"

"Eight years, plus the half year I stayed with Michelle."

"Eight and a half years. That's a long time. You must have liked your job."

"Oh, absolutely!" And she continued, "Scotty was only one year old when I started to work for Mr. and Mrs. Lamont, and I got attached to him."

"Did you know that Steven Lamont had an affair?"

She looked at me disapprovingly and replied, "No. And it would have been none of my business."

I had not taken the draft letter to this meeting, but I decided to tell Teresa of its existence and of what was written in it. She listened carefully and then shook her head.

I asked, "You have no idea what the draft was referring to?"

"No, Ma'am."

"Can you enlighten me of who Shelby is?"

"No, I don't know any Shelby."

I looked at her intently and then said, "Mrs. Cesar, you've got to understand that I'm not prying into the Lamont family's private matters because I'm nosy. It is my job to investigate a possible reason for their murder."

She nodded and said, "Yes, I understand."

I continued, "I've interviewed a few family members and so far, no one has been able to tell me anything about a person by the first name of Shelby. No matter who this Shelby was, it seems to me that Mr. Lamont had been discreet about the relationship."

On a hunch, I asked, "Did you know or suspect any extramarital relationship on Mrs. Lamont's part?"

She took a long time before she reluctantly replied, "I'm not sure."

"But you suspected that she had an affair?"

"Yes."

"Do you know who the man was?"

She waited even longer with this answer and then murmured, "I suspected the politician."

I said, "The politician? Do you mean her brother-in-law, Luke Sosna?"

She nodded and said, "I can't be sure. And it really was none of my business, anyhow."

I looked her in the eyes and stated, "I know it was hard for you to tell me this. I promise you, unless this has a direct impact on my investigation, it will go no further."

Then I asked, "How did you first learn of the tragic accident?"

"Michelle called me in Panama," she replied.

"Michelle seems to be an interesting young woman."

"Oh yes! She is very smart, but she never talked down to me. We had a good time together those six months, just her and me."

"She told me you got married. Are you still doing domestic work?"

"Not anymore. I started a little business. I work out of my home."

"What kind of business?"

"I make silk flower arrangements for weddings and other special occasions."

"Oh, how interesting!" I exclaimed.

Then I said, "By the way, Scott said, 'Hi,' in case I should run across you."

Her big brown eyes lit up, and she said, "Dear Scotty! How is he?"

"He is an extremely independent boy, determined to find out what happened to cause his parents' death," I said.

Teresa Cesar stated, "I understand that he wants to know. But I don't like it."

Chapter 9

Relaxing in our recliners that evening, Peter looked up from his book and asked, "How is your pro bono case coming along?"

"Well," I mused, "I've learned some interesting things from the people I've talked to so far, but all that information is hard to sort out."

"You feel like unburdening yourself?"

"Sure," and I told him all I had discovered, starting with my call to Sergeant Wolf. When I got to my interview with Michelle Lamont, Peter asked, "What sort of a young woman is Michelle?"

"A very interesting one," I replied.

"What's her major?"

"Philosophy."

Peter inquired, "Where is she planning to go with that?"

"Oh, she'll take it somewhere, I'm sure."

As my narrative came to an end, Peter stated, "Yes, you've learned a lot already. But does it get you anywhere, I wonder?"

I replied, "As I said, I've got to sort all that information out."

"Who else are you planning to talk to?"

"Tomorrow I'll drive to Orange County and pay Nicki and Vicki a visit."

"Sounds like the Bobbsey twins!"

I continued, "Then on Wednesday I have a lunch date with Rachael Moreley, the late Mr. Lamont's secretary."

"You have the next two days neatly cut out for yourself," he commented.

After a pause, he said, "Has it occurred to you, Regula, that the Lamonts' fatal crash could have been nothing more than an accident?"

I winked at him and said, "There's always that slight possibility!"

Before I went to bed, I made a list of what I had learned from each person:

Scott Lamont: Had found a draft letter written by his father to someone named Shelby, presumably his mistress, the day before the fatal crash. In it was stated that something occurred and the late Mr. Lamont was flying to L.A. to investigate and get proof.

Michelle Lamont: Told me she heard her dad shout at someone on the evening before his attempted flight to L.A. The argument could have been with someone in the house, or he might have been on the phone.

Suzanne Prescott: Informed me that Luke Sosna was a congressman. I also learned from her that the Sosnas were spending their two-week stay at Tahoe starting this week. I further learned that Claire Lamont had decided at the last moment to join her husband on that flight because she needed to see her dentist immediately.

Thomas Teleford: Told me that originally he was going to be his partner's passenger on that flight, before Claire's last-minute decision.

Teresa Cesar: Told me that she suspected Claire Lamont had an affair with Luke Sosna.

I stared at my list for a while. I had learned a few interesting facts from these people, but nobody seemed to know who Shelby was.

Chapter 10

My appointment to meet with Nicki and Vicki Prescott was at 2:30 p.m. I had plenty of time to work out at the gym and come home and shower before I had to take off for Orange County. Thus refreshed in body and mind, I was on my way by noon. I wasn't especially familiar with Irvine, but since the apartment building I was looking for was in close proximity to the University of California, finding it was effortless.

The window stood open, so even before I rang the bell, I heard music and laughter coming from inside the apartment.

A bubbly young woman opened the door and said, "Oh, is it two-thirty already? You must be R.A. Huber. I'm Vicki. Come on in."

As I was ushered inside, several young people of both sexes squeezed by me on their way out.

I addressed Vicki and said, "I hope I'm not interrupting anything?"

"Oh no," she replied, "we were rehearsing our parts for a play, but everyone was just starting to leave. Have a seat while I straighten up a little."

Looking around me, I realized that the room was a mess. Some furniture was upside down, torn bits of papers were scattered about giving the effect of confetti, and a stepladder was placed horizontally in the center. I presumed this was all part of a stage décor.

I watched Vicki as she "straightened up." It looked to me more like shoving things aside. She was fun to observe. Her blondish, straight hair was spiked out in all directions. Her eyes were blue, and she sported a little round button nose. It was obvious the young woman had been more than generous with applying make-up. This all made for a "happy clown" effect.

"That's better," she commented, and pulled a chair up to face me.

I said, "Thanks for taking the time to talk to me."

"No problem. I had no classes this afternoon." And she added, " My sister should be here soon."

I inquired, "Who is older, you or Nicki?"

"I'm the baby," she giggled.

"So you're a freshman. Correct?"

"That's me!"

"What will you major in?"

"Liberal Arts."

Waving my hand at the items in the room, leftovers from the "stage scene," I said, "So you are planning to become an actress?"

"No. I'm just taking a drama class this semester. I don't know yet what I'll end up doing," she replied.

At that instant the door was flung open and Nicki made her entrance. She resembled her younger sibling, but her make-up was not quite so dramatic, and her hair was not spiked. She looked surprisingly orderly.

She dropped into a chair and said, "I hope I'm not too late for all the excitement!"

Puzzled, I said, "Excitement?"

She stated, "I've never been questioned by a private investigator before. I was thrilled when you called and said you wanted to talk to us!"

I laughed and said, "I hope you won't be disappointed. Detective work is not always thrilling. As a matter of fact, it can be tedious at times."

Then I said, "Vicki and I were just discussing her major. What is yours, by the way?"

"Social Ecology."

"You're in your sophomore year?"

"Yes."

"Do you know what professional line you'll take?"

"I don't know yet, but I have plenty of time to decide," she stated.

Then I said, "Okay. Let's get to the reason I came to see you both. You know that I'm investigating the plane crash of your Uncle Steven and Aunt Claire."

Nicki said, "Too bad we don't know anything about it, though."

"What do you remember of your uncle and aunt?"

Vicki said, "I don't understand what you mean."

"What impressions did they make on you, if any?"

"Oh, I see. Uncle Steven was cool. We didn't see him often, but we always had a lot of fun with him up at Tahoe. He was a fantastic skier."

Then Nicki put in, "I'll always remember him as Santa."

I asked, "Santa Claus?"

"Sure. When we were little, he dressed up as Santa and gave us kids presents. I never let on, but I always recognized him because of his green eyes."

"What do you remember about your Aunt Claire?"

Vicki said, "She was nice too, but more reserved."

Then I asked, "Do either of you know anybody by the first name of Shelby?"

They both shook their heads.

I told them about the draft letter. They seemed more surprised than shocked about its existence.

Nicki commented, "Wow! Uncle Steven had a mistress!" And her sister said, "I'd never have guessed!"

"So you have no clue who Shelby is?" I asked.

"No," they both said in unison.

"Do you have any idea what your uncle wanted to investigate?"

"No," they stated.

"When was the last time you saw your aunt and uncle alive?"

Vicki replied, "Up at Lake Tahoe, of course."

"I mean, specifically, on what day?"

Nicki said, "I remember. It was the day before the plane crash. We were all skiing and boarding together. Then we broke up after lunch and did our own thing."

I inquired, "Did either of you see your uncle or aunt that evening?"

They looked at each other and shook their heads.

After a pause, I stated, "That's all the questions I had." And I added, "I take it you both enjoy college life?"

Nicki commented, "We love it. There are parties every weekend."

"And sometimes even during the week!" said Vicki.

Driving home, I reflected on the conversation I'd had with the Prescott girls. Their chosen majors were interesting; it occurred to me that neither of these young women was worried of having to make a living in the near future. So I had learned that Nicki and Vicki were having a ball at college, but the interviews certainly did not bring me any closer to my task of finding out why, if indeed, Mr. Lamont's plane had been tampered with.

Chapter 11

Rachael Moreley and I met during her lunch hour at the *Purple Saucer*, located in the general San Fernando Valley area. I got to the restaurant first and was ushered to a reserved table for two. Looking around me, I was amused by the décor. The color purple was predominant. From tablecloths, napkins and breadbaskets to lamps, walls and ceiling, everything was done in different shades of purples. Even the pictures hanging on the walls had purple frames.

Soon, Ms Moreley, led by the hostess, turned up. I got to my feet and as we shook hands, I surveyed her briefly. I was looking at a woman in her forties. Her medium brown hair was cut short in a no-fuss style. She was clad in a dark striped double-breasted suit, a white blouse and a pair of black Oxford shoes. Glancing at her light-brown eyes, I realized I was being sized up and scrutinized.

The waiter took our orders, a Caesar salad for Ms Moreley and a chef's salad for me.

After he was out of earshot, I commented, "I hope our salads will be mostly green, and not purple!"

She laughed. "This must be your first time at the *Purple Saucer*. I come here often and don't even notice the purples anymore. I work right around the corner, so this place is convenient for me."

I said, "Thanks for coming."

She replied, "Frankly, my first reaction when you called was to tell you I was not interested in meeting with you. Then I guess I got curious." And she added, "I doubt that I can help you, though."

"How long had you been working as Mr. Lamont's personal secretary when the tragic plane crash occurred?"

"I worked for Steven Lamont a total of nineteen years. When he started his brokerage firm there were only three of us: Mr. Lamont, James Bradley, the accountant, and me. For the first several years I took care of all office work, except bookkeeping. Then, as the business prospered, the office staff got bigger and I became Steven Lamont's personal secretary."

The waiter brought our salads, and although served on lavender plates, I was happy to find the food in its natural color. We concentrated on eating for a while.

Then I commented, "You must have enjoyed working for Lamont & Associates. Nineteen years is a long time."

"Yes," she replied, "I liked working for Steven Lamont. He was a fair employer and easy to get along with."

"Did you ever take any lengthy breaks from the job, like for example maternity leave?"

Ms Moreley replied, "No. I never had any children. I was never married for that matter. I'm a lesbian. My partner and I went on vacation trips over the years, but those travels never took me away from the job for longer than a month."

After a pause, I asked, "At what point in time in the company's history did Thomas Teleford come on board?"

She reflected and then said, "That was about five years prior to Mr. Lamont's plane accident. Steven Lamont had hired two brokers over the years, but as the business expanded even more, he felt the need for another senior broker besides himself, so Thomas Teleford joined the company as a partner."

"After the tragedy, were you offered another job at Lamont & Associates?"

She shook her head. "I guess I could have stayed and tended to the secretarial needs of the two junior brokers, but frankly, after having been Steven Lamont's personal secretary for so many years, that just didn't appeal to me."

"Yes, that's understandable." And I added, "There was no question of you becoming Thomas Teleford's personal secretary at the time?"

She grinned and said, "Mr. Teleford likes to make a statement with the physical appearance of his secretaries! I'm not sure whether this is for his own enjoyment or to impress the clients."

I smiled and said, "Yes, Monique seemed decorative."

"I don't know Monique. She must be his latest secretary. They were all 'decorative,' like you say. He changed secretaries four times in the five years I knew him. Don't get me wrong. He also insisted on them being efficient, besides the look."

"Did you resent Mr. Teleford for that?"

"Oh no! To each his own," she said.

Then I inquired, "Is the bookkeeper, I think you said James Bradley was his name, still with the company?"

"No. He retired just around that time."

"Did you know Mrs. Lamont?"

"Yes, but not well. I saw her seldom, mainly at the company's Christmas parties. She was always pleasant on those occasions."

"How about the children? Did you ever meet them?"

She replied, "I saw even less of them. I met them at a company picnic once. The boy was about six at the time, and the girl might have been in her early teens."

Then I stated, "I've talked to several family members and no one was able to tell me the reason Steven Lamont suddenly cut his vacation short at Lake Tahoe. I hope you can enlighten me about that."

"I really have no idea."

"He had no pressing business that you knew of?"

"No," she said, "but he called me from the Truckee airport that morning and said he was on his way back to L.A."

Surprised, I said, "He did? What exactly did he tell you?"

"He didn't give me the reason for coming down. He just told me that he was planning to stop by the office. Oh, and by the way, he also wanted to know if James was still there."

"The accountant?"

"Yes."

I said, "I don't understand. What did Mr. Lamont mean by 'if the accountant was still there?'"

"James Bradley was retiring that same week, so Mr. Lamont wanted to know if he'd already left."

"Ms Moreley, I know this might be hard four years later, but please try to remember Mr. Lamont's exact words when he called you on that fatal morning."

She thought about it and then stated, "I can't remember word for word, but he said something like this: 'Hi, Rachael. Something came up and I'm returning to L.A. immediately. I'm at the Truckee airport and will take off shortly. I'm stopping by the office. Is James still there? I'd like to talk to him. See you soon.'"

"What did Mr. Lamont sound like?"

She stared and then said, "I am sure it was him and not an imposter."

"No, what I meant was, did he sound his normal self, or did he sound upset?"

"Oh. I see what you mean now." And after thinking it over, she said, "He sounded more like he was in a hurry to get down here."

Then I questioned, "Did you think his main purpose in coming back was to talk to the accountant?"

"I don't think so."

"What was your impression?"

She answered, "I might be wrong about this, but my feeling was that he had pressing business in the area and also planned to come into the office. He might have just wanted to say good-bye to James since he was down here anyhow."

"I see." Then I said, "Was the accountant still there, by the way?"

"He hadn't arrived at the office yet when I received the call, but he got there a couple of hours later. His last day was the following day, Friday," she replied.

"Do you happen to have Mr. Bradley's phone number? I'd like to get in touch with him."

"He moved to Central Mexico shortly after he retired. I don't have his number, but I can give you his address. We exchange Christmas cards."

"I'd appreciate that very much."

Then I inquired, "Do you know anyone by the name of Shelby?"

She stated, "The only Shelby I know is Thomas Teleford's daughter. Why do you ask?"

Amazed, I said, "Out of all the people I have questioned so far, you are the first person that knows anyone by that name."

"I don't understand. You told me on the phone you had been to see Thomas Teleford, and you actually got my number from him. He knows perfectly well he's got a daughter named Shelby!"

"Actually, my time with Mr. Teleford was limited, and so he was the only person I forgot to ask who Shelby might be. Now I'm kind of glad I didn't ask him."

She looked at me, somewhat exasperated, and then inquired, "What's all this fuss about Shelby?"

I decided after all the valuable information this woman had given me, I owed her an explanation. I reached into my purse, took out the draft letter that Scott had found, and handed it to her.

She read it carefully and then commented, "Wow! I can imagine that Thomas Teleford would've been less than pleased had he known about this. I always thought that Shelby was a bit scared of him."

"How did you know Teleford's daughter?"

"She worked at Lamont & Associates one summer."

"Did you know she had an affair with Steven Lamont?"

She shook her head and said, "This note you just showed me was a big surprise. I had no idea."

I probed, "Did the rest of the draft letter suggest anything to you?"

After a pause, she said, "Maybe I was wrong with my impression that Steven Lamont planned to come to Los Angeles on a business matter. This bit in the note to Shelby, 'it might make a difference in our relationship,' suggests something of a private nature."

"It might," I said.

Then I asked, "Did you by any chance stay in contact with Shelby? I would prefer not to ask her father for the phone number."

"No, sorry. I'm not in contact with her. I think she studied to become a teacher, but I have no idea where she lives and teaches."

I looked at my watch and said, "You're probably anxious to get back to your job."

"Yes, I'd better be going."

I thanked her for her time and the valuable information. She promised to call with James Bradley's address. After she left, I lingered amid the purple surroundings a while longer, thinking about the dialogue we'd just had. Then I paid the bill and went on my way.

Chapter 12

Back at my office, I felt sure I was going to find Shelby Teleford without any outside help, provided she lived in Southern California.

When I started my detective agency, I had collected a great selection of phone books. So I leafed through the various directories: Los Angeles, Pasadena, Glendale, Burbank, San Gabriel Valley and San Fernando Valley. I came across Thomas Teleford, but no Shelby.

She might have an unlisted number, I considered. As a last resort, I picked up the phone book with Orange County listings. And there she was!

I checked my watch; it was 3:45 p.m. A schoolteacher would probably be home by 4:00 p.m., I presumed. I waited 15 minutes, and then made the call. Ms Teleford seemed bewildered when I requested an interview but consented to a face-to-face talk with me on Friday after work.

On my drive home to Merida, I was itching to share my "find" with Peter. Traffic was moving along slowly, so I mulled over the past 18 months to pass the time. I knew Peter had been skeptical when I first started my sleuthing business. True to his passive nature, however, he did not try to stop or discourage me. When I actually had tucked some success under my belt, he started to show an interest in my cases. Especially the previous two, I mused.

Peter had a lot of insight. Amazing how he could sometimes state the obvious, and, without knowing it himself, point me in the right direction.

Once home, I found my hubby hacking at his computer in a writer's frenzy. He barely took time out to eat his dinner. Obviously, he felt the need to put his thoughts down as fast as they came into his head.

I realized that sharing my case with him that particular evening didn't lie in the cards.

Chapter 13

Household chores and errands kept me busy all Thursday morning, so when I finally made it to my office in Pasadena, it was already afternoon. I heard the phone ring before I unlocked the door, and I made a dash for it.

Rachael Moreley was on the line and, true to her word, gave me James Bradley's address in Mexico.

I called international directory assistance, and after a lot of repeating and spelling out words in Mr. Bradley's address, I got the number and then dialed it.

"Aló?" said a female voice.

I said, "Quisiera hablar con el Señor Bradley."

"Un momentito por favor."

The *momentito* turned into a very long moment.

Then I heard a male voice, "James Bradley here. Who is this?"

I introduced myself and explained the reason for my call.

He heard me out and then asked, "What do you mean, you're investigating the Lamont plane crash?"

I said, "It might not have been an accident."

"You're suggesting foul play? That's absurd! Who would've wanted to harm Steven and Claire Lamont?"

"I aim to find out."

He declared, "I'm having a hard time digesting what you just told me. But even if it were true, how can you possibly be successful with your investigation four years after the fact?"

"By tracking backward and digging," I replied. "I hoped that you might be able to help me."

"I don't see how."

I continued, "I've learned that Mr. Lamont had planned to fly to Los Angeles to talk to you on that fatal day."

"Who told you that?"

"Rachael Moreley. I had lunch with her yesterday. She was also the one who gave me your address, by the way."

"Good old Rachael!" And he asked, "I wonder what made her think Steven Lamont was on his way to see me that day?"

"Apparently, he called her just before his attempted flight. He asked her if you were there, because he wanted to talk to you."

"I see."

"Did Ms Moreley tell you Mr. Lamont was expected at the firm that morning, after she received the call?"

"No. And even after the plane crash, she didn't say anything about his call. Come to think of it, under the circumstances, what would have been the point?"

I inquired, "Do you have any idea what Steven Lamont wanted to discuss with you?"

"I can't think of any reason in particular," he replied. And after a pause he said, "I was retiring the very next day. Maybe he just wanted to say good-bye to me."

"Yes, that's a possibility."

Then I continued, "I understand, just like Ms Moreley, you worked for Steven Lamont nineteen years. You must have been a loyal and trustworthy employee."

He said, "I was, and Steven Lamont was a just and generous employer. He offered me a pension when I took early retirement."

"Oh, you retired early? May I ask how old you are?"

"I'm 66 now. I was 62 then," he said.

"In your opinion, what was the reason Mr. Lamont cut his ski vacation short and planned to fly home?"

"I have no idea."

"How do you like life in Central Mexico, Mr. Bradley?"

"I love it!"

"I thought you might," I said, and we ended the call.

I was just ready to lock up and leave when Maryanne Sosna called to let me know she and her husband were willing to talk to me.

Things were moving right along, I thought.

Chapter 14

On Friday afternoon I ventured out to Orange County once more. Shelby Teleford lived in Huntington Beach, and following the directions she had given me, I found her apartment fairly easily.

The young woman who greeted me at the door was tall with dark hair like her father, but her eyes were blue. She wore a peasant blouse tucked into a flower-print cotton skirt, reaching down to her ankles. There was an aura of innocence about her. She led me into a dinette part of the kitchen and motioned me to the table.

Shoving aside a large pile of papers and books, she said, "Excuse the mess. I just got home a few minutes ago." And pointing at the stack, she added, "These are my students' tests. I'll be spending a good part of the weekend correcting them."

I asked, "What grade do you teach?"

"Fourth," she replied. And she added, "I love teaching at that level. The children are so eager to learn at that age. They're not distracted by hormonal changes yet."

Then she looked at me intently and stated, "I was a little confused after your phone call. What exactly are you trying to investigate about the Lamont accident, and what does it have to do with me?"

"The plane crash might not have been an accident."

Her eyes opened wide, and she said, "You don't mean someone killed them on purpose?"

I nodded, "Yes, it might have been murder."

"That's horrible!" And after a pause, she added, "Who gave you my name and number?"

I replied, "I got your name from Rachael Moreley. I looked the number up in the phone book."

"Rachael Moreley? Why would she give you my name?"

"Let me explain. I only had a first name, Shelby. No one could tell me who this Shelby was. Then I interviewed Ms Moreley, and she was able to give me a last name to go with the first."

She shook her head and said, "I still don't understand."

I took the draft letter out of my purse and, handing it to her, I said, "This is a draft. Did you ever receive the finished product?"

She read the note carefully. Then she read it once more.

Handing it back, she said reflectively, "So Steven actually had attempted to write me a letter."

"You never received one?"

"No, but he called me from the Truckee airport early that Thursday morning, March 2, just before he started his flight."

"What did he say?"

She replied, "Oh, basically the same thing that was written in the note you just showed me."

"Please try to remember his exact words. It might be important."

She took a moment, then stated, "He caught me just before I was leaving for a class at college, and if I remember correctly, he said he'd started to write a letter, but was concerned it wouldn't reach me by the weekend. He told me that he was cutting his trip short and would be returning to Los Angeles that very day. He sounded pretty upset, as I recall. I was concerned because he said that some serious emergency had come up that he needed to look into right away, and that it could affect our relationship. He told me he'd call me on Friday or Saturday because he wanted to see me that weekend and that he'd explain more to me then."

I said, "Were you and Steven Lamont lovers?"

She bent her head and said, "It sounds sordid, but yes, we were."

After a pause, she asked, "Where did you get that draft letter?"

"Scott Lamont found it in his late father's desk at Lake Tahoe about two weeks ago."

"Oh, how sad! The boy must be upset to have found out about his father's infidelity in that way."

"Actually, he seemed more interested in the rest of the statements made in that note." And looking at her searchingly, I asked, "What did you make of Steven Lamont's call to you, just before the tragedy?"

She replied, "I was hoping he had found out that his wife was cheating on him, and that he might consider marrying me." And she added, "That was wishful thinking on my part, of course."

"Before that phone call, had Mr. Lamont ever suggested to you that he suspected his wife was having an affair?"

"No."

"Did he ever give you reason to believe that someday you might become more than his mistress?"

"Not really."

I changed the subject and said, "I understand that you worked for Lamont & Associates. When was that?"

"It was the summer of my junior year at college."

"Was that the summer before the plane crash?"

"Yes, it was."

"Who hired you?"

She said, "I'm sure you know that my father was Steven's partner."

I nodded.

All of a sudden, it seemed Shelby Teleford had the urge to unburden herself, and she spilled out her story: "My dad and I were never close. My parents got divorced when I was in elementary school. I lived with Mom and saw Dad only occasionally. He has a forceful and authoritative personality, and consequently I was never at ease around him.

"On one of his rare visits in spring of my junior year at college, I told him I was looking for a summer job. When he offered me work with Lamont & Associates, I knew I didn't really want an office job. What I had in mind was a position of some kind working with children. He insisted it would be great to see each other more often, and I had the feeling it was an attempt on his part to have a better father-daughter relationship. So I accepted his offer and worked at the brokerage firm that summer.

"One day towards the end of the summer job, I questioned Dad about something I came across in my data entry. He snapped at me and said, 'Don't try to be clever and understand things that are obviously way above your head. Just do your job of data entry.' That really hurt my feelings, and Steven Lamont walked in on me as I was crying bitterly, bent over on my desk with my head buried in my arms. Steven was sweet and understanding. He calmed me down, and I remember him saying, 'Don't take life so seriously, Shelby. At your age, you should have fun.' And he made a clown face and sang, '*Life is just a bowl of cherries!*'"

She smiled at this recollection, and then continued, "After that day, he started to take an interest in me. At first it was more like a fatherly concern, and then things just happened. I fell deeply in love with him. We didn't actually have a relationship until after my summer job at Lamont & Associates was over and I had gone back to school. We had to be careful and discreet. Steven never picked me up at my apartment. We usually met in the park, and then he took me someplace, either in his car or, occasionally, in his plane. We didn't get together nearly as often as I would have liked, but Steven was extremely busy with his job, and he was also dedicated to his family."

As her narrative came to an end, I realized I might have been the first person she ever vented her story to.

I asked, "Did anyone know of your affair?"

"I'm sure nobody did. We were very careful."

"Were you so discreet because of Steven Lamont's wife and kids?"

"Yes, partly that. But mostly I was terrified of my father, should he find out."

I said, "I see." Then I asked, "Had you met Claire Lamont?"

"No. I'm glad we never met. That would have been hard for me."

"Did Steven talk to you about his wife?"

"Seldom. He never said anything negative about her, if that's what you mean. In his own way, Steven was loyal to her."

"Did he talk about his children?"

"Occasionally. He adored them."

"Did you ever meet his daughter or son?"

"No."

Then I asked, "Who informed you of the tragedy?"

She said, "I read it in the paper Friday morning. I totally fell apart. I didn't go to classes and cried the entire day. The worst thing was that I couldn't talk to anyone about it. Thank God I had read it in the paper first. When Dad called me with the news Friday night, I could at least fake a somewhat normal reaction. Had I learned it from him firsthand, I probably would've given myself away."

"I can understand that was a tough time for you." And I added, "How would you feel now, if your father found out about your affair with the late Mr. Lamont?"

She smiled and said, "It wouldn't be tragic for me anymore. It's a thing of the past. I'm also no longer afraid of my dad." And she continued, "I was very young then. That doesn't excuse anything, I know. Having the affair was wrong."

I had noticed an engagement ring on her finger, and pointing to it, I said, "I see there is someone else now!"

A happy expression came over her face, and she replied, "Yes, I'm engaged. We're getting married in July."

"Congratulations!"

I thanked her for all she had shared and then left her to the task of correcting the students' tests.

Chapter 15

Peter knew that I would be driving home from Orange County in rush-hour traffic. We had dinner plans at *Chez Tante Jeanne* and left the time open. I was moving at a snail's pace along the 405 Freeway, and when merging onto the 605 North, I knew that dinner wasn't going to be early. Over an hour later, on the 210 West, and finally close to the Pasadena area, I reached for my cell phone. I told Peter to meet me at *Tante Jeanne's* in half an hour's time.

He was waiting for me outside the restaurant and had a "near starvation" look on his face. On entering, Maurice greeted us with his usual, "Nice to see you both," and led us to our favorite table. After a brief study of the menu, I decided on a Quiche Lorraine, and Peter ordered *Tripes à la mode de Caen.*

Winking at me, he said, "I've had a craving for tripe for months!"

There are few things I refuse to cook, but tripe is at the top of the list.

We ate in agreeable silence. The cuisine at *Chez Tante Jeanne* was always excellent, and since we were extremely hungry that evening, the food seemed to taste even better than usual.

Over coffee, at the end of the meal, Peter said, "So what's up?"

I replied, "You were so busy writing the last couple of days, I never had a chance to bring you up to date about my case."

"Well, I'm all ears now!"

I stated, "I didn't learn much from Nicki and Vicki, other than their late Uncle Steven's eyes had been green, and that there was a lot of partying going on in their lives. Rachael Moreley, on the other hand, gave me valuable information. She's in contact with the former accountant of Lamont & Associates, and gave me his current address. He lives somewhere in Central Mexico.

"And," I paused for effect, "I found Shelby, thanks to her!"

"Attagirl!"

"Shelby turned out to be Thomas Teleford's daughter!"

"The partner's?"

"Yes."

He asked, "So your drive to Orange County today was to pay a visit to Shelby Teleford?"

"None other."

"What was she like?"

"I did not know what to expect, but actually, I had a favorable impression of her."

Then I proceeded to tell him all about my conversation with Shelby, leaving nothing out.

At the end of the story, Peter asked, "You've met her father. Is he really the tyrant he sounds?"

"No, not really," I said. "He gave the impression of being authoritative and business-like, but I didn't judge him as being nasty or unkind." I added, "I think Shelby is a sensitive young lady and I imagine she gets her feelings hurt easily."

Then he stated, "So your visit confirmed that there actually is a person named Shelby and that she was the late Steven Lamont's mistress. However, it seems to me the lady was no big help in solving the mystery of what Steven Lamont was going to investigate, given the chance."

"True."

Then he said, "I wonder why Lamont kept that draft letter in his desk? I mean, since he changed his mind and wasn't going to mail her any letter, why not toss the draft?"

I reflected and then said, "My guess is he was interrupted while writing the note. Maybe his wife or someone came into the room. So he might have shoved it into the secret compartment of his desk, with the idea of retrieving it later."

"Yes, that's possible."

We didn't speak for a while, and then I asked, "How do you feel about taking a little trip with me?"

He laughed, exclaiming, "Don't tell me you want to take your pro bono case all the way to Mexico, Regula!"

"No. I took care of the Mexican connection with a simple phone call. I had something a little closer and colder in mind. How about a few days of skiing?"

"Sort of combining business with pleasure?"

"Something like that."

He thought about it for a while and then announced, "Oh, why not? Apart from a couple of local trips to Big Bear, we haven't done any skiing this season."

"Great! There is still tons of snow at all the ski resorts in North Shore Tahoe. I checked it out on the Internet."

"When are we going?"

"How about Sunday?"

"You mean the day after tomorrow?"

"Of course! Aren't you excited?" I said.

Chapter 16

We spent most of Saturday gathering ski equipment and packing our bags. Since the little trip did not include a weekend, I had no trouble finding accommodations. I made a five-night, Sunday through Thursday, motel reservation near Kings Beach, at North Shore Lake Tahoe. We called our son and daughter, respectively, to inform them of the spontaneous ski trip. I also decided to let Scott Lamont know.

Once on the line, he said eagerly, "Did you find anything out?"

I could picture the boy's expectant face clearly and answered, "Lots of things, but they all need to be sorted out. An investigation like this, especially four years later, takes time, Scott."

"Oh, I know. I just want to make sure you're still working on it." And he added, "You must be running out of money by now. I asked Michelle, and she'll pay your fee."

Laughing, I replied, "You are determined I should get paid!"

Then I said, "The reason I'm calling is to let you know that my husband and I are driving up to Lake Tahoe tomorrow."

"Cool! So you're going to check out the crime scene!"

"Well, I would not call it that, just yet. No crime may have been committed. But, yes, I will pay the Truckee airport a visit."

"What else are you going to do?" he asked.

"I plan to talk to your Uncle Luke and Aunt Maryanne. And I'm planning to get some skiing in, as well," I replied.

"Oh! You ski?"

"I certainly do!"

"How about boarding?"

"Heavens, Scott, I'm too old to try that!"

Chapter 17

The journey was about a nine-hour drive, so we left our house at 7:30 a.m. on that Sunday, March 21. We took turns driving, with Peter taking the first stretch. Still on the 210 West, only ten minutes into our drive, he started his cross-examination.

I knew it was coming, so I was not surprised when he said, "Do we have everything?"

"Yes, Peter, we do."

"Did you remember the chains?"

"Yes, sir."

He turned his head, checking the back of the SUV, saying, "Is my boot bag here?"

I said, "Okay. I'll tell you exactly what's in the car. Just concentrate on driving." And turning around, I announced, "I see two pairs of skis and poles, two boot bags, a big suitcase, a small suitcase and two carry-ons. Our jackets are folded over the suitcases."

He said, "Better to make sure now than in a few hours."

"Right," I agreed.

Then, yawning, I commented, "I got up unnecessarily early." And closing my eyes, I promptly dozed off.

When I woke up, we were heading north on Interstate 5. I surveyed my hubby for some time and thought that although his hair had turned white, and his chin sagged a little, Peter still posed an agreeable picture. The prominent eyebrows and mustache remained dark. His hazel eyes held strength of character, which I found comforting.

Suddenly, he turned his face toward me and said, "What are you staring at?"

"Oh, nothing. I was just thinking that gray hair looks distinguished on a man, but I'm not sure whether the same applies for a woman."

"Well," he chuckled, "I'm thankful to be of the male gender, then!"

We lunched at the Harris Ranch Restaurant, halfway between Los Angeles and Sacramento. Harris Ranch is a San Joaquin Valley landmark. The ranch raises the finest beef on the West coast as well as a variety of fruits, vegetables and nut crops. Peter thoroughly enjoyed his Cajun beef tips, and I savored the Rueben sandwich set before me.

After the lunch stop, it was my turn behind the wheel. We soon left the open field of ranch cattle behind. The pistachio and almond trees beside the highway were in bloom, presenting a pretty picture of pink and white for miles. For the most part, however, the landscape along I-5 was boring, so we inserted a Rod Stewart CD to keep awake.

I was driving through Sacramento, merging onto the 80, when Peter asked, "Want me to take over?"

"No, I'd rather keep going. If we should get into a snowstorm further up and have to don chains, I'll let you drive."

After passing the town of Auburn we were climbing steadily, and as we headed for the Donner Pass, I couldn't help but think of the tragic fate the Donner Party had endured when trapped in the Sierra Nevada Mountains in heavy snowstorms so many years ago.

Peter said, "You're thinking of the Donner Party, aren't you?"

"Yes, I always do along this road," I said.

Then I wondered, "They came along Truckee Lake and the river. How come they didn't fish? I mean, I'm sure they had tools they could have used to cut out holes on the frozen lake."

"I assume there was a huge bank of snow on top of the frozen lake, and I can imagine they didn't even realize there was a lake underneath."

"Oh, I hadn't thought of that."

Luckily for us, the road was clear and there was no trace of an approaching storm in sight.

As we were nearing our destination, I stated, "Maryanne Sosna told me to call once we'd get to the area."

He commented, "So, Regula, it turns out this trip was not as spontaneous as you made me believe!"

"Maybe not," I said.

Chapter 18

We rose early the following morning, consumed a continental breakfast at the motel, and headed for the slopes. It had snowed during the night, so we were in for a treat of fresh new powder. The streets were clear, though. Apparently the snowplows had already been put hard to work. We decided on Northstar for our first day of skiing. This resort was conveniently close to our motel in Kings Beach, and since we had plans to meet with the Sosnas that evening, we didn't want to venture too far and be pressured for time at the end of the day. Besides, I wanted to keep my favorite, Squaw Valley, for later in the week.

We found a spot in one of the parking lots relatively close to the entrance, an indication that Northstar wouldn't be crowded on that particular Monday. Changing into our boots and shouldering the skis, we walked through Northstar village. "Village" is an exaggeration, but I call it that, for lack of a better word. There are some shops and restaurants, lockers, and the ticket booths where one buys the lift tickets.

On our way up in the gondola, I looked out on the vast winter paradise and felt elated to be there. I surveyed the terrain below us and judged I was looking at about six to eight inches of fresh snow on top of a generous base. I kept staring into the unspoiled whiteness. Peter had apparently said something, but I was deep in thought and did not pay attention.

He nudged me and said, "Hey, Regula! Are you with me?"

"Sorry," I said, and I tried to explain my train of thought. "I just wondered if one could still detect any of the old tracks hidden below the new powder, by sweeping the top layers away. That's silly, of course!"

Peter shook his head and said, "You come up with the strangest things!" And he added, "I take it you're dwelling on the Lamont case?"

I nodded.

Chuckling, he stated, "If anyone can find old tracks from four years ago, I'd bet my bottom dollar on you!"

"Thank you."

Leaving the gondola, we passed the main lodge, donned our skis and took the short Arrow Express chair lift to connect us with the Comstock Express further up.

Once arrived at the summit, Peter suggested, "Let's do some runs at the east ridge first. We can do the other side of the mountain in the afternoon."

"Okay, I follow you," I said.

We were skiing along the ridge when Peter suddenly stopped and said, "We should take advantage of the virgin powder and take an ungroomed run. How about it, Regula?"

"It's a lot of work, but let's go for it," I agreed.

We each made our own tracks in the soft blanket of whiteness, sinking in so deeply that the snow nearly reached our knees. There was a sense of total union with nature, skiing in deep, unspoiled powder. It was tricky, however; there is a lot of skill involved in ungroomed snow, especially when making turns. On the groomed runs, Peter and I were equals, but when it came to virgin powder, Peter was the champ in the family.

I didn't detect the mogul underneath the fresh snow, until I was on - and over - it, and I took a tumbler. The fall was as soft as landing in a down featherbed. Digging myself out was hard work, however. By the time I was finally back on my feet, Peter was long gone. I skied in his tracks for a short time, and then I decided I had had enough and traversed through the woods, parallel with the mountain, until I merged onto a groomed run.

Peter was waiting for me at the bottom of the lift and said, "What a cute, white, snow-bunny you've turned into!"

We took the Comstock chairlift back up. From the summit the view of the surrounding mountain range, and the valley with Lake Tahoe below, was absolutely breathtaking.

We skied the east side of the mountain that morning, exploring some black diamond runs, like *Grouse Alley*, *Crosscut*, *Tonini's* and *The Chute*.

While eating lunch at the lodge, Peter exclaimed, "What a glorious day! We have perfect snow conditions and beautiful sunshine. I'm so glad you 'made' me come!"

I grinned and said, "Me too!"

In the afternoon we tackled the back side of the mountain. On our way to the summit on the Backside Express chairlift, I pointed below and asked, "What mogul run is that, directly under us?"

"I think it's *The Rapids*," Peter replied.

"Well, let's stay away from *The Rapids*. That would be too hard on our knees."

The back side proved to have steep, long, and partly challenging runs. We both experienced quite a rush on some of those steep and long stretches. At 4 o'clock, we just made it to the chairlift for one last ride up before it closed down for the day.

As we walked to our car, we felt this had been a day well spent.

Chapter 19

We were expected at the Sosnas' at 5:30 p.m. for après ski cocktails. Arriving at the motel, there was just enough time for a quick cleaning up and a change of clothes, but not for showers.

Driving along the lake on highway 28, Peter commented, "I'm surprised they invited us both." And he added, "And for cocktails, no less! I'm sure they're aware of the fact that this is not a social occasion."

I said, "They know we are on a ski trip and are combining it with an interview. In Maryanne Sosna's circles, it might be considered bad etiquette to only ask one person over, knowing that the spouse is in town also. Come to think of it, she might like to make it a social event, rather than an investigation."

As directed, we found the residence in a small community, halfway between Kings Beach and Tahoe City. There were three similar A-Frame houses grouped in a cluster, erected near the lakeshore. A driveway led down to all of them, then separated into three individual alleyways. According to the numbers, the one in the middle proved to be our destination. We parked in front of the garage, and then rang the doorbell.

A well put-together woman opened the door and, motioning us inside, said, "Hello. You must be Mr. and Mrs. Huber. I'm Maryanne Sosna." And as we followed her through an entryway, down a short hall, and into a room that was presumably the family room, she continued, "As you can see, we are casual up here."

We were introduced to Luke Sosna. He was wearing a pair of khaki Dockers and a navy polo shirt. His salt and pepper hair was cut short, and his gray, intelligent eyes looked out at the world with benevolence, it seemed. Maryanne Sosna must have been referring to her husband with her remark about being casual. There was nothing remotely casual about her appearance. Her makeup was applied to perfection. She wore a light blue silk pantsuit, high heels, a double strand of pearls around her neck and pearl earrings. The color of the suit enhanced the deep blue of her eyes. Her ash-blonde hair was kept in a stylish do, which looked simple, but I knew took great pains to achieve.

Stepping over to the bar, Sosna said, "Have a seat while I fix the drinks. What do you like? I have pretty much everything at hand: scotch, gin, vodka, rum, tequila, wine, beer."

We accepted margaritas, and I said, "Please make mine weak. I'm the designated driver."

The lady of the house had a Martini & Rossi Sweet Vermouth, and Sosna poured himself a scotch and soda. Drinks in hand, Peter and I sat in comfortable upholstered chairs facing our hosts, who were seated on the black leather couch.

Mrs. Sosna inquired, "Where did you ski today?"

"At Northstar. The new powder was absolutely tops," I said.

The congressman put in, "We just came back from Homewood a little while ago. The conditions there were also excellent."

At that point I decided it was time to cut the small talk, and I said, "I appreciate that you agreed to talk to me about the sad event of four years ago." And I added, "Is your son here, by the way?"

Our hostess answered, "Yes. He's in his room with a friend. I think they're playing games. Is it necessary that you talk with him? I'm sure he can't tell you anything more than we know."

I replied, "Don't bother him right now, but I would like to have a word with him later."

Then she said, "My sister told me about the letter Scott found. I'm astonished and shocked at what it implies."

"Which part?"

"All of it!"

"You did not know of your brother's affair?"

"I had no idea."

Then I addressed Mr. Sosna and stated, "I understand you skied together with Steven Lamont the day before the plane crash?"

"Yes, until lunch," he said.

"Did he mention his decision to fly to the Los Angeles area the following day?"

"No. Actually, we had plans to ski at Squaw Valley together the next day."

"Can you think of anything that prompted Mr. Lamont to cut his ski vacation short and attempt that flight?"

He shook his head and said, "No."

I continued, "Did you know that the original plan was for Thomas Teleford to join Steven Lamont on that flight?"

"No, I wasn't aware of that."

"His wife decided at the last minute to take Mr. Teleford's place," I said.

The congressman exclaimed, "So Claire was on that plane by a fluke of fate! Oh God!"

His spouse gave him a sharp look and then said, "Didn't I tell you at the time? Claire called me early that Thursday morning. She told me she was sorry, but I had better find a replacement for her in the fashion show. She had a horrible toothache and was going with Steven to Los Angeles to consult her dentist."

Her husband said, "You didn't tell me!"

After an awkward pause, I asked, "When was the last time you saw or talked to your brother-in-law?"

He replied, "I saw him for the last time the day before he died. It was in the morning while skiing at Northstar. No, I take that back. I saw him again for just a moment at the end of the ski day, when we all gathered before walking to the cars. We also talked briefly on the phone that evening."

"Please tell me what the phone call was about. It might be important," I said.

"Oh, it was unimportant. Soon after coming home from skiing, I called him to see if I should go over to his place to play a game of *Go*, the Japanese board game. The ladies were busy in this house planning Maryanne's fundraiser, and I felt that I was in the way. He said he was sorry, he couldn't. Apparently he ran into someone at Northstar and was going to have a drink with that person before dinner."

I inquired, "Did he say who that person was?"

"I didn't ask, and he didn't say."

Then I turned to his wife and asked, "How about you? When was the last time you talked to your brother?"

The lady replied, "I was busy with organizing my charity fundraiser at the time. I did not ski that Wednesday at all." She reflected for a moment and then said, "I saw and talked to him last on Tuesday, when we were all skiing at Mt. Rose."

"This fundraiser you were planning, was it going to be held in Washington, D.C.?"

"No, we were having it right here," she answered.

Surprised, I said, "You were planning a fundraising event at Lake Tahoe? How extraordinary!"

"It was my one and only fundraiser here, and not particularly successful. Let me explain. I do volunteer work for several charities. I'm in charge of organizing annual fundraisers. That particular year I tried something new by having it during the week of the Lake Tahoe snowfest. There is a snow festival held every year during the first week of March with fireworks and all sorts of sporting-and-entertainment events. I planned a dinner-fashion show featuring ski outfits for women, men, and children, as well as après ski outfits.

"As I said, it didn't turn out to be a success. Even though I purposely set the cost low, at only $50.00 a plate, I came to realize that people traveled here mainly for skiing and maybe a little gambling and nightlife, at most. A charity dinner-fashion show was not on most folks' agendas."

In total amazement, I said, "You mean you didn't cancel the event, learning of your brother's crash?"

"It was too late to cancel," she replied.

I stared, and noticed that Peter stared at her too.

Looking at us both in turn, she apparently felt the need to explain further and stated, "The event was planned for Friday, the very next day. Tickets had been sold, the food had been ordered, and caterers were hired. Most of the models and help had been volunteers, but two professional runway models were scheduled to fly in that Thursday evening."

I said, "I see."

Then she commented somewhat defensively, "As you can imagine, I was not in the best frame of mind during the event, but I had to go through with it."

I felt it was best to change the subject, and turning to the congressman, I asked, "Was Steven Lamont an experienced pilot?"

He replied, "He was conscientious about safety matters, if that's what you mean, but he hadn't been flying all that long."

Peter, who had been silent until then, asked, "How do you know he was conscientious?"

"I was with him during a few of his flights."

"Oh, you're a pilot too?" Peter inquired.

"Yes. I was actually the one who introduced him to flying." And with a remembering smile, he added, "He got hooked on it pretty fast. He bought the Cessna 152 while in training. A few days before the accident, he told me he was ready to upgrade to a bigger machine. He planned to buy a Beechcraft Bonanza."

Peter said, "Do you own an aircraft?"

"Yes. I have a Twin Cessna 310."

I asked, "Do you fly to Truckee when you come here to ski?"

"Yes, always."

"I'm planning to pay the airport a visit. It might be too much to ask for, finding someone still there who worked at the place four years ago, but I'll give it a shot."

Mr. Sosna stated, "You're in luck. Bill Mc Naught is an old hand at the airport. He's sort of a legend at Truckee. He was a mechanic and retired years ago, but he loves planes and still hangs around and actually makes himself quite useful."

"I'll look for him, then," I said.

At that instant we heard voices sounding from above, and a second later, running feet chasing down the stairs. The door partially opened, and a boy of about sixteen or seventeen stuck his head in.

He said, "Sorry to interrupt." And looking at his dad, he asked, "Can we borrow the car? We're hungry."

"Come in for a minute, Chris," Mr. Sosna said.

Introductions made, the boy looked at Peter and me expectantly. Chris had inherited his gray eyes from his father and the full mouth from his mother, but the boy's hair made a totally independent statement. Spiked out, and alternately colored in layers of black and blonde, it was left to the beholder to perceive either a zebra or porcupine effect.

His mother said, "Mrs. Huber wants to talk to you."

"Awesome! You're the private investigator, right?" And with a gleam in his eyes, he added, "I didn't think I was going to be let in on this!"

Amused at his enthusiasm, I said, "Your parents are very helpful with my investigation, but I'd like to ask you a few questions as well."

"Shoot," he said.

"How old are you?"

"Seventeen."

"You're a senior in high school?"

"Yes."

"So at the time of your uncle's plane crash, you were 13."

"Uh-huh. Now I wish I hadn't been such a kid then and had kept my eyes open." Then he burst out, "Was Uncle Steven really murdered?"

"I don't know; I'm trying to find out," I said. Then I continued, "I understand that you and your cousin Scott went snowboarding on your own the afternoon before the tragedy."

He nodded.

Then I asked, "When did you see your Uncle Steven last?"

He thought about it, and then said, "I saw him at the end of that day up at Northstar, when we all met to head back to the cars."

"What do you remember best about your uncle?"

"You mean what kind of a guy he was?"

"Yes."

"He was fun. I miss him when we're up here."

I said, "Thank you, Chris." And with a little wink, I added, "You can go eat now, if that's okay with your parents."

Mr. Sosna looked at me and asked, "Are we almost done?"

"Yes, just about."

He turned to his son and said, "We'll go out for dinner together, if you boys can just wait a few more minutes."

"Sure, Dad."

He said good-bye to Peter and me and was out the door.

I addressed the congressman and said, "I only have one more question, and then we won't intrude on you any longer. This might seem irrelevant to you, but I'd like to form an accurate picture of your brother-in-law's last day. Michelle told me that you had all scattered after lunch, and skied in separate little groups. She did not mention, however, that you all gathered at the end of skiing. I learned from her that her mom and her Aunt Suzanne went home after lunch to help your wife with preparations for the fundraiser. So, getting to my question, in whose car did the two ladies leave, and who drove away in which cars at the end of the day?"

After a pause, he answered, "If I remember correctly, the ladies took the Prescotts' car home after lunch. At the end of the day, we had two cars left in the parking lot. Steven drove Keith Prescott, Michelle and Scott home, and I loaded my car with Nicki, Vicki and Chris."

"Thomas Teleford was not skiing with you?" I inquired.

He replied, "Thomas was there that year. He skied with us the day before at Mt. Rose, but I don't remember seeing him on Wednesday at Northstar."

Mrs. Sosna put in, "I remember. He did not ski that day at all. It was his last day before flying home, and he took his girlfriend shopping in Reno."

"You have an excellent memory, Mrs. Sosna," I complimented her.

Then Peter and I thanked them for their hospitality and got up to leave.

Mr. Sosna accompanied us out of the house. The stars above shone brightly, and the moon reflected against the mound of snow piled up on each side of the driveway. I could also easily discern the two residences on either side of the Sosna home in the bright moonlight.

I commented, "It's peaceful and quiet out here." And motioning in both directions with my hands, I asked, "Which is the Lamont house?"

Sosna stated, "The one to your left, and the other belongs to the Prescotts." He added, "They're empty at the moment, of course. I wish our family had been here with the others this year. I miss the hustle and bustle usually created by all the cousins getting together."

I asked, "Was your trip delayed because your wife was holding a fundraiser in Washington, D.C.?"

"Oh no. Maryanne is good at planning her events around our trips. I'm afraid I was to blame for this year's delay. There were several important congress meetings which I could not afford to miss." And winking at me, he stated, "After all, I have a duty to the taxpayer!"

We thanked him again, slid inside the SUV, and drove away.

Chapter 20

As I steered out of the driveway and turned onto Highway 28, Peter said, "I don't know about you, but I'm starving. Why don't we drive over to the Nevada State line, have dinner, and then do a little gambling?"

"Sounds like a good plan," I agreed.

I concentrated on the road, making sure I didn't spot any ice. The surface looked perfectly clear and dry.

I remarked, "You didn't say much at the Sosnas' house."

"I felt my role was that of a silent observer."

"I see. And what were your observations?"

"It was interesting to see you in action, Regula."

"What action? I thought the meeting was rather tame."

He said, "I guess so, but I never joined you on any interviews before, so it was a new experience for me."

"I have to take you along more often!" Then I said, "Seriously, what did you think of them?"

"They seem a pleasant couple and I found them extremely cooperative."

"What else?"

"They seem to have remarkably good memories."

I said, "Yes, that's true. But under the circumstances that's natural."

"How do you mean?"

"When someone close to you dies, you usually make a point of remembering the last times spent with that person."

"You're right about that." Then he said, "Something else is interesting."

"What's that?"

He chuckled and said, "The fact that Sosna plays *Go!*"

"Ah! I knew you'd tuned in on that. It wouldn't have surprised me if you had asked him to play a game with you!"

"I was tempted." Then he asked, "What did you make of them?"

"Well, I haven't met any politician in person until tonight, but I didn't expect someone in Luke Sosna's position to be as open and obliging as he turned out to be."

"I'm sure during the course of his career he learned that it is more effective to treat his adversaries with honey rather than vinegar."

I continued, "I might do her an injustice, but Maryanne Sosna struck me as superficial and plastic. Amazing how she got herself looking the way she did, at the end of a skiing day! And did you notice her nails?"

"Her fingernails? What was wrong with them?"

"That's just it, they were perfect!" I replied.

Peter said, "Now, Regula, are you getting catty in your old age?"

"Not at all. It just amazed me. While on a ski trip, my nails always look a mess. With all the buckling and unbuckling of boots, the sliding in and out of gloves, I just assumed everyone's nails would suffer." I went on, "Anyhow, looking at Mrs. Sosna, I couldn't help but comparing her with her sister. They are remarkably different. Suzanne Prescott is a down-to-earth chubby little redhead, full of vitality."

Then I said, "What did you think of the interviews?"

He replied, "We learned quite a bit. Do you suppose Mrs. Sosna was aware of the affair between Claire Lamont and her husband?"

"Hard to say. The look she gave him, when it seemed to occur to him for the first time that Claire had been on that plane by a chance of fate, could be interpreted in two ways."

"I've lost you."

I said, "The look could have meant, 'I know of the affair and you still seem to care about her' or it could have simply meant, 'I thought I told you about Claire joining Steven on that flight.'"

"Oh, I see what you mean now."

Then I said, "Unless Sosna is an extremely good actor, he did not know until today that Claire Lamont's presence in that plane was a last minute decision. He also claims ignorance about the initial plan for Thomas Teleford to have been on that plane."

"Which means?"

"If Luke Sosna is our murderer, he meant to kill only Steven Lamont. Unless he is lying about not knowing ahead of time that anyone else was joining Lamont."

"So the same goes for Mrs. Sosna."

"Yes, except she admits to having known early that morning that Claire Lamont was on the plane. So she could have meant to kill either or both of the Lamonts."

Then Peter said, "What about this person who met Lamont for a drink before dinner? Do you think he had something to do with the crime, if there was a crime committed, that is?"

"You called that person a 'he' but we don't know the sex of that individual. Sosna didn't say." And I added, "I hope I can find that stranger, if he or she exists."

"You think the person was made up by Lamont?"

"That would be a far-fetched possibility. I was thinking that the individual could have been invented by Sosna." Then I said, "I need to question Michelle about it. She was with her father the entire day of skiing. She might remember if her dad ran into someone he knew. Maybe sitting on a chairlift or something."

Peter asked, "Do you think Lamont learned from that person whatever it was that prompted him to fly to Los Angeles?"

"Possibly."

Then he commented, "Mrs. Sosna seems to take her volunteer jobs extremely seriously. Incredible that she did not cancel that fundraiser."

" 'The show must go on' type of woman."

We drove in silence for a while, and then he asked, "What was your point in questioning who went in whose car at the end of the day?"

"I basically wanted to get a clear picture of who was around Steven Lamont that last day of his life." And I added, "This whole mystery amounts to what Mr. Lamont learned, and from whom, that made him abandon his ski trip and go to Los Angeles."

At that point we had arrived at the California/Nevada State line.

In our motel that night and already under the covers, Peter stated, "What an eventful day!"

Joining him, I asked, "How did you do at the blackjack table?"

"I came out just about even. How did you fare?"

"I should have quit while I was ahead. I did real good shooting craps, but ten minutes later, I gave it all back to the house."

"Easy come, easy go," he said.

I was just dozing off when he remarked, "I noticed you smoked in the casino. What happened with your patch?"

"I couldn't stand it anymore with everyone puffing away around me, so I took it off and joined the crowd."

"You've done real good with cutting down on this trip, Regula. I'm proud of you!"

"Yeah, yeah," I murmured, and lost consciousness.

Chapter 21

We got up late Tuesday morning, and after breakfast Peter asked, "Are you headed for Truckee today?"

"I sure am. Want to come along?"

"No, thanks. I have other plans."

"At which ski resort do you want to be dropped off?"

"For once you're reading me wrong, Regula. I'm planning to stay put right here at the motel."

Astonished, I said, "By yourself?"

"Just me and my laptop," he replied.

Laughing, I said, "Leave it to you, Peter! How did you manage to smuggle it along? As far as I know, I did all the packing."

"That's my secret," he said.

I first went on a brisk walk down to the lake and back for a little exercise. Also, I did not want to get to the airport too early since I planned to catch Bill Mc Naught at his lunch hour, if I could locate him, that is. The crisp air felt good, and I breathed in deeply. Down by the water, I was enchanted with the view of the mountains surrounding the lake. I could see South Lake Tahoe at the opposite shore. I bent down, picked up some snow and formed it into a snowball, then tossed it as far into the lake as possible. I guess I'm a kid at heart.

At 11:30 a.m. I drove away, taking highway 267 for the short ride to Truckee Tahoe Airport.

Once there, I walked up to the operations desk on the second floor of the terminal.

"Can I help you?" the young airport staff man asked.

"I hope so," I said. "I'm looking for Bill Mc Naught."

"He's here, but I think he's doing some minor repair right now. Is he expecting you?"

"No. He doesn't know me, but I'd like to have a word with him. When does he take his lunch break?"

The young man stated, "Bill takes his breaks whenever he wants."

I reached into my purse and extracted my card. Handing it to him, I said, "If you could see that he gets this, I'd appreciate it. There's no hurry. I can wait until he's available."

He read my business card aloud, "R.A. Huber, Private Detective." Then he looked at me and said, "I hope Bill didn't get himself into trouble."

"Oh, not at all. I just need to discuss something with him."

The man said, "Have a seat," and vanished behind a door.

He soon reappeared, saying, "It might take a while before Bill Mc Naught can see you."

I smiled and said, "I don't mind waiting. I came prepared," and I took a book out of my bag and started reading.

Several people came and went to the operations desk with their respective requests, while I sat patiently and killed time.

Then a little old man pushed through a side-door and briskly made his way toward me. I was so startled by his looks that I probably stared open-mouthed. The wrinkled fellow, with his pointed ears and a mischievous glint in his eyes, looked precisely like a leprechaun!

Before I could utter a word, he hollered in a high, squeaky voice, "So what's your business with me, lady detective?"

I got up, extended my hand and said, "Nice to meet you, Mr. Mc Naught." Then, looking around the room, noticing the young staff man as well as several other folks eyeing us expectantly, I added, "Can I take you out to lunch, please?"

Chuckling, he said, "Sure. I'm always up for a free lunch!"

I drove him to the charming little town of Truckee, just a mile or two away. Truckee resembles an old mining town, with its western storefronts and the train tracks running through it.

As we reached the town center, I stated, "Your choice. Where do you like to eat?"

He picked a little coffee shop, and I found parking less than half a block away.

When seated, a middle-aged waitress came to our table and jokingly said, "So you've found yourself a date, Billy!"

After she was out of earshot, I said, "Maybe we should have chosen a place where you are unknown?"

Grinning he stated, "No such place in Truckee."

"You're that well known? I'm impressed!"

"I've lived here most of my life, and then some."

I ordered a turkey sandwich and the waitress then turned to my "date" to ask, "The usual for you, Billy?"

He nodded. Then addressing me, he questioned, "So what's this all about?"

"I'm investigating a plane accident that happened four years ago."

"On your card it said 'private detective'. It didn't mention the NTSB."

"I'm a private investigator, and not from the National Transportation Safety Board."

"I don't understand."

At that point our food arrived, and I refrained from explaining further. To my amazement Billy's "usual" was a vegetarian platter. He must have noticed the surprise in my eyes.

He laughed and said, "What did you expect? Corned beef and cabbage?"

I liked the man's sense of humor and spunk. He obviously had turned his peculiar looks to his advantage long ago.

As soon as the waitress left us, I said, "Let's get back to our subject. How long have you worked at the Truckee airport as a mechanic?"

"Forever! I'm retired now, but like to think I'm still useful."

"I'm looking into the plane crash of Steven and Claire Lamont."

He raised an eyebrow and said, "The NTSB investigated that accident, and as far as I know, the report was finalized years ago."

"Yes, I know. I was hired recently to investigate the matter. The crash might not have been accidental."

He looked at me perplexed and said, "You mean foul play?"

I nodded.

After a pause, he asked, "Are you working for an insurance company?"

"No. I was hired by a family member."

"Oh."

Then I inquired, "Did you know Steven Lamont?"

"Of course," he replied.

"Were you working at Truckee Tahoe Airport in the days before and on the day of the crash?"

"Of course."

"Mr. Mc Naught, please tell me everything you remember about Steven Lamont and his plane, from the time he landed at Truckee to the time he took off on that fatal day four years ago."

He took a few seconds to think and then stated, "On the day Steven Lamont landed his Cessna 152, he told me he needed an oil change done and - -"

I interrupted, "Please tell me exactly what he said."

"Okay. He said something like, 'The engine is due for an oil change. Can you take care of it, Bill? There is no hurry; I'm staying for two weeks.' Then he told me that the next time I saw him up here, he'd be in a Beechcraft Bonanza."

I asked, "Where was the plane parked while at the airport?"

"In an assigned spot, but I can't remember in which number, exactly," he replied.

"Did you get around to doing the oil change before Mr. Lamont took off earlier than expected?"

"Let's see. I think I did so about three days before his departure."

"What about refueling? Was that done on arrival or before departure?"

"He tanked up on arrival."

Then I asked, "Was Mr. Lamont alone when he came up?"

"No, his boy was with him," he said.

"Oh, Scott flew up with his dad. I didn't know that." And I added, "Was that the first time you met his son?"

"Oh, no. His father brought him along a couple of times before. He was a curious little guy. When I first met the boy, he wanted the engine explained to him!"

"I can picture him doing that," I commented. Then I asked, "Do you remember anything unusual during the time Mr. Lamont's Cessna 152 was parked at the airport?"

Baffled, he said, "Should I?"

I clarified, "Did you see anything or anyone suspicious around the plane or airport?"

"Oh, I see what you mean. Offhand, I can't remember seeing any strangers, or anyone suspicious hanging around."

I continued, "Now we're coming to the day of his departure. Did you see Mr. and Mrs. Lamont then?"

"Oh, sure. It was morning."

He stated, "I was ready for a little break around 9:00 a.m. I had poured myself a cup of coffee from the vendor machine at the terminal when Steven Lamont came out of a phone booth. I was surprised to see him so soon, and he told me that he was taking off for Van Nuys in a few minutes. I informed him that the oil change was done. His wife came out of the lady's room and they went outside. About ten minutes later I saw him take off."

"Did Mr. Lamont explain to you why he was leaving earlier than planned?" I asked.

"Nah."

"How did he look to you?"

"I don't know what you mean."

"Was he happy or sad, worried or angry, his usual self or different?"

"Oh, I get you now." He reflected and then stated, "He might have been upset, but I had the feeling he was mostly in a hurry to get going."

"What about Mrs. Lamont?"

"She looked like she was in pain."

I questioned, "When you did the oil change, did the Cessna look in good running condition to you?"

"Absolutely."

"You mentioned that at 9 o'clock you took a break. How early do you start work?"

"I don't have a schedule. It's pretty much left up to me when I want to come and go. On that particular day, I started at around seven."

I took a moment to reflect on what else I should ask the mechanic and then said, "Did Mr. Lamont mainly fly to Truckee in winter for the family's ski trips, or did he come up on other occasions as well?"

He answered, "He hadn't been flying all that long; it was only his second winter at the time of the crash. He came with his family in summer, and he made lots of little trips up during the year, staying only a day or two each time. I remember he flew here often while in flight training and only stayed long enough for a bite to eat and to refuel."

"So you got to know him well," I said.

"Oh, I knew him even before he was flying on his own. His brother-in-law, Mr. Sosna, used to take him along."

"I see. When Mr. Lamont flew up on the short trips, did he come by himself, or did he take passengers along?"

"Sometimes he was by himself, and other times he had company."

"Do you remember the people he occasionally brought along?"

He pouted and said, "Sure I do. You know what lady? You're rather nosy!"

"It comes with the job."

With a smirk he stated, "If you expect to hear that he took any mysterious passengers along, you're out of luck. The people I saw him bring were his wife, his daughter, his son, his brother-in-law, his partner, and his flight instructor. One at a time, of course, the Cessna 152 being a two-seater."

I said, "I understand Mr. Lamont was going to upgrade to a bigger plane, a Beechcraft Bonanza, I think you mentioned. Would that have been comparable to the aircraft Luke Sosna owns?"

"Not quite. Mr. Sosna has a Twin Cessna 310, which some say is a step up from the Beechcraft Bonanza. Mr. Sosna is here right now, by the way; I noticed his plane parked in the lot."

"I know. I talked to him yesterday," I commented. And I added, "I'm under the impression Mr. Sosna has been flying for a long time."

"Oh, yeah. I remember him flying to Truckee for at least ten years, maybe longer."

"I understand Mr. Teleford's plane is a Beechcraft also."

He clarified, "Teleford's is a Beechcraft Baron, which is in the league with the Twin Cessna 310. The 310 and the Baron are about the same; they're both six seaters."

"Do you fly, Mr. Mc Naught?"

"Nope, never learned how, but sure love to be around planes."

"I think it's time I dropped you back to your flying machines, then," I joked.

He said, "With all the fancy talk we had, I doubt it helped your murder investigation."

"Maybe not," I said, "but I sure enjoyed the lunch date!"

Chapter 22

At dinner that Tuesday evening, Peter inquired, "So did you have a productive day?"

"Not really," I said, "but I had a date with a century-old Leprechaun!"

He stared and then said, "You say the weirdest things!"

Then I gave him a short version of my encounter with Mr. Mc Naught.

At the end of my saga, Peter said, "Is he really as elderly as you make him sound?"

"Bill Mc Naught cannot be called 'elderly' by any stretch of the imagination. He's *old!*"

"You got lots of information out of your Leprechaun, but none of it helps you much, does it?"

"No such luck," I said.

Then I mused, "Lamont was extremely careful where he took his mistress. He apparently never showed up with Shelby at the Truckee airport, and I would imagine he never took her anyplace where there was the slightest risk of running into an acquaintance."

Peter commented, "It seems he was able to keep his affair a secret. A small wonder in today's world!"

"Exactly."

Then I stated, "One thing is sure. Claire Lamont definitely seemed to have had a toothache the day of the crash. Mr. Mc Naught, who did not know the purpose of her flying to L.A., observed that she looked like she was in pain."

Surprised, Peter said, "You didn't believe that before?"

"I take nothing for granted."

Then he considered, "The plane seemed to have been in order when the mechanic changed the oil, three days before Lamont took off. So we can assume that if someone fiddled with the plane, it would've had to be done within that timeframe."

I mulled this over for a moment. "I don't think the three-day timeframe matters."

"How come?"

"From the beginning I've taken it as fact that the reason Steven Lamont cut his vacation short was because of something he learned during his stay at Lake Tahoe. Then, after questioning the family members, I was convinced that whatever he discovered he hit upon the day or the evening before the tragedy."

Peter said, "Yes, of course. So it doesn't matter how many days that plane sat parked at the airport after the oil change. If it was sabotaged, that would have been done that night."

"Correct. Or the next morning, the actual day of the crash," I pointed out.

"Do you think you might get results from questioning other personnel at the airport?"

"I doubt it. Whatever could be learned at the Truckee airport was noted by the NTSB in their initial investigation, I would presume."

He nodded.

Then I stated, "Our attempt at discovery at Lake Tahoe is over, I'm afraid. Once back home, I'll have to sit and think. In the meantime, we have two more days of skiing left!"

"Isn't that the main reason we came?" Peter teased.

"How is your book coming along?"

"Pretty good, but I can't think of a catchy title."

"I could probably come up with something witty, if I knew what the story is all about!"

"Good try, Regula, but no dice!"

Peter had this odd rule of never letting me read any of his manuscripts before the books were published. So far, all my attempts at altering this resolve had failed.

I said, "Speaking of dice, do you feel lucky? Shall we indulge in a little gambling tonight?"

"Let's skip it tonight. All that hard brainwork made me tired! We want to get up early tomorrow and be on the slopes as soon as the lifts open." And he added, "How about turning in early and just fooling around?"

"You're not too tired for that?" I asked, mockingly.

Grinning he said, "Never!"

Chapter 23

The next two days we spent skiing. We explored Alpine Meadows on Wednesday and kept the best, Squaw Valley, for our last day in the winter wonderland.

Peter woke me up at the crack of dawn on that Friday, March 26, saying, "We'd better hurry up and get out of here. There is a storm brewing, and I want to avoid having to don chains."

I am not an early riser by nature and prefer to start my day in a leisurely fashion. When pressed, however, I can adjust.

I opened one eye and mumbled, "Okay. I'll try to hustle."

When I came out of the shower, Peter handed me a cup of coffee freshly brewed from the machine provided by the motel. In another 15 minutes we were both ready and loading the SUV with luggage and ski equipment. While Peter walked to the office to check out, I looked up at the sky and was aware that, indeed, a major storm was imminent.

It wasn't even 6:30 a.m. yet when we drove away from the Lake Tahoe area.

Peter said, "Let's get down the mountain first and then stop for breakfast someplace, maybe Auburn or even further down."

"Okay with me," I said.

By the time we reached the Donner Pass, the first snowflakes started to fall. Luckily for us, the storm moved in the opposite direction and was soon left behind.

After breakfast, Peter teased, "Are you awake enough now to get behind the wheel?"

"Sure, if you can keep me stimulated," I shot back.

We had been driving in silence for a long stretch when Peter commented, "Are you thinking about the hidden tracks?"

"Yes," I said, "tracking backward is even harder than I expected."

"Is there anyone you can eliminate?"

"At this point, I suspect everyone."

"You can't seriously suspect the boy of being the culprit!"

I asked, "Chris Sosna?"

"No, I meant Scott," he said.

"Scott is the only exception, of course."

"Because he was too young at the time?"

I stated, "That's not the reason. He hired me and caused me to make waves. This was a dormant crime, if committed. The murderer would not want to stir things up."

Then he said, "Have you thought about motives?"

"Yes, but they are not obvious. Until we find out the reason for Lamont's flight to L.A., it's pretty useless to try to come up with motives."

Peter said, "Luke Sosna might have wanted to prevent him from finding proof about his affair with Claire. Nowadays, politicians are pretty vulnerable in that department."

"I thought of that. But Lamont might have learned something that day which could have been equally detrimental to any of the others."

After a pause, he asked, "How are you going to proceed with the investigation?"

"I'll talk to Michelle, and hopefully she'll remember the person Lamont ran into. I also need to find an expert who can give me an idea of how the plane could have been tampered with. Beyond that, I'll play it by ear."

We did not mention the case anymore for the rest of our journey home.

Chapter 24

In my office Monday morning, I opened up the Lamont file and leafed through the contents. It was dismayingly sparse. Besides the note to Shelby, the NTSB report, and the names, addresses and phone numbers I had gathered, it only held the comments I had entered after the first few interviews. So far the list consisted of what I had learned from Scott Lamont, Michelle Lamont, Suzanne and Keith Prescott, Thomas Teleford and Teresa Cesar. I now added,

Nicki and Vicki Prescott:	Learned that one majored in Social Ecology, the other in Liberal Arts. They both agreed Uncle Steven had been cool.
Rachael Moreley:	Lamont called her from Truckee airport telling her he would come into the office. Lamont also wanted to talk with James Bradley. Learned that Shelby was Teleford's daughter.
James Bradley:	Did not know what Lamont wanted to discuss with him. Took early retirement and was pensioned by Lamont & Associates.
Shelby Teleford:	Lamont called her from Truckee airport and basically told her the same thing as is

stated in the draft, with the addition that he would see her that weekend and call her Friday or Saturday. She confirmed that they had been lovers. She was sure nobody knew of the affair.

Luke Sosna:

Didn't know Thomas Teleford was originally going to be on that flight. Did not know Claire Lamont took his place. Showed great surprise and distress when I mentioned that fact. Lamont told him that he ran into someone and was planning to have a drink with that person the evening before the crash. Learned that Lamont was a conscientious pilot.

Maryanne Sosna:

Claire informed her early that morning of joining her husband on the flight. Did not see her brother at all the day before the tragedy. Went ahead with the fundraiser scheduled for the day following the crash.

Chris Sosna:

Was enthusiastic about my investigation and regretted he had been too young to keep his eyes open four years ago.

Bill Mc Naught:

Made an oil change to Lamont's Cessna 152 three days before the crash. Learned that Lamont was in the process of upgrading to a Beechcraft Bonanza. The plane had been refueled on arrival. Did not see any strangers or anyone suspicious hanging around the Cessna 152. Noticed Lamont come out of phone booth at airport around nine o'clock on fatal morning. Saw him take off ten minutes later. Said Claire Lamont looked like she was in pain. Stated plane was in good running condition when oil change was done.

I stared at the list for a long time. So much information, and I was still in the dark. Frustrating! Then I picked up the phone and dialed Michelle's number.

"Hello?"

"Oh, Michelle! This is R.A. Huber. I was going to leave a message; I didn't think I'd find you at home."

"I don't have any classes today until one o'clock. Did you find out anything new at Tahoe?"

I replied, "I learned a few new facts. I'm trying to sort them all out. I have a couple of questions for you."

"Sure, go ahead," she said.

"Do you remember the exact dates when you arrived and left Tahoe four years ago? This might not be important, but I'd like to add it to my records."

After a pause, she answered, "I don't remember the exact date we got there, but I think it was a Tuesday. The plan had been to stay the usual two weeks, but after what happened to Mom and Dad, we all cut our stay short, of course."

I stated, "I have an Almanac in front of me. I'm looking at the year in question. Could it have been Tuesday, February 22, when you arrived?"

"Yes, I remember now. We flew up Tuesday the 22nd and had planned to stay until Tuesday, March 7. We all flew home on Friday after the crash, except Aunt Maryanne and Uncle Luke, who stayed for the fundraiser that Friday."

Then I said, "I learned that Scott flew up with his dad. Did you and your mom drive up, or did you board a commercial flight?"

"We flew commercial into Reno."

"How did you get to Tahoe from there?"

"The Prescotts got there first, so Uncle Keith picked us up. Whoever was there first always picked up the others at the airport. Mom went to fetch Dad and Scott at Truckee later."

"I don't think I understand," I said.

"I guess I didn't make myself clear. Each family keeps a four-wheel-drive at Tahoe. The first family arriving would take a shuttle bus or a cab to the house. Then the rest would get picked up by whoever was there first. Of course, the years before Dad knew how to fly, our family flew together on a commercial flight. After he became a pilot, he loved flying so much that he always came up in his own plane."

"Oh, I see." Then I asked, "Did Scott always go up in your dad's plane?"

"No, we took turns. Dad was going to buy a bigger plane so that the whole family could go together on future trips."

I could hear the sadness in her voice when she uttered the last words. I said, "I'm sorry I have to stir up memories for you, Michelle."

"Oh, they're good memories. It's okay."

"Did your dad plan to fly back to Tahoe after his business was taken care of in Los Angeles?"

She paused and then said, "I never thought about that. I doubt it. We were all scheduled to go home the following Tuesday."

"Your Uncle Luke mentioned that your father had run into an acquaintance on his last day of skiing. Mr. Sosna did not know who that person was, however. Since you spent that entire day with him, can you remember anyone he met while skiing?"

"I don't think so," she replied.

"Think hard, Michelle. This may be important. For example, he might have known someone you sat with on a chairlift together."

"Really, I don't recall him talking to anyone but the family." Then she exclaimed, "Wait, there was somebody. I remember now! It was at the end of the day. We were waiting at our usual meeting place by the ticket counter at Northstar before heading to the cars. I had to use the restroom, and when I got back to Dad he was talking to a man."

"Do you remember what was said?"

"Apparently they were finished talking when I showed up."

"Do you know the man's name?"

She said, "Dad introduced us, but I can't recall his name now."

"Tell me exactly how your dad introduced you. Maybe the name will come back," I suggested.

"He said, 'This is my daughter, Michelle.' Then he turned to me and said, 'meet - -' it's useless. I can't remember the name."

"Maybe it will come back to you. Don't worry about it," I said. And I added, "Did the three of you talk together, then?"

"No, but Dad and the guy made arrangements to meet later for a drink. I didn't pay much attention because I saw the boys, Scott and Chris, headed our way."

"So your dad and his acquaintance did not exchange any other words?"

"No, the man said good-bye to me, and 'See you later' to Dad, and left."

"Would you recognize him again?"

"I think so," she said, "I'm sure I had never seen him before or afterwards. I wish I could remember the name. You obviously think it's important." And after a pause, she mused, "His first name was something common, like 'Ralph' or such. His last name might have been French, but I really can't recall."

"Don't trouble yourself about it anymore."

Then she asked, "Did Scott tell you I'm paying your fee? Please send me a statement including your expenses at Tahoe. I'll stop by your office and sign a contract next time I'm in your neighborhood."

"That is very generous of you. I'll take you up on it, except for the trip to Lake Tahoe. My business up there would have taken no more than a day. My husband and I made a ski vacation out of it, which we thoroughly enjoyed, by the way."

Chapter 25

While munching on the sandwich I had packed, I mulled over the next step to take. I could not come up with any rational plan of action. Ready to give up, I suddenly said to myself, of course! Why didn't I think of that right away? Then I reached for the phone.

"Hi Peggy!"

"Well, hello Regula! How are you?"

"Just fine, thanks. Actually I need Walt's help."

She said jokingly, "First I don't hear from you in ages, and then you want my husband! You're a fine friend!" And she continued, "He won't be home until after four. What do you want him for?"

"I need his expertise."

Surprised, she asked, "You need a financial adviser?"

"No," I replied, "I need a pilot. This has to do with a case I'm working on. He still flies, correct?"

"Sure." And she asked excitedly, "Are you chasing someone and need Walt to fly you in pursuit of that person?"

I laughed and said, "No, Peggy. Nothing as dramatic as that! I just need some facts about airplanes."

"Oh, is that all," she said, clearly disappointed.

"If I swing by your house on my way home, do you think Walt could give me an interview?"

"Of course, and you're allowed to say 'Hi' to me too!"

"Thank you!"

As we hung up, I asked myself, had I really neglected Peggy lately? She seemed to think so. The last time we had spent a day together was in January, on Super Bowl

Sunday, to be exact. It had long become a tradition between us to have an outing that particular day while the men watched their ball game. Amused, I thought back to her choice for our ladies' day out this year. She had wanted to go ice-skating, and so we had spent the afternoon at the skating rink. Both of us hadn't done any skating for at least 35 years, and the endeavor had turned into a daring adventure.

My mind still remained on my friend. Peggy and I had been pals ever since our kids were little. The husbands got on well too; after all, they had a common interest in football. It never failed to amaze me how two so completely opposite personalities like Peggy and Walt could have ever found each other. Peggy was barely 5'2" but oh, what a fireball! She was a flamboyant, energetic extrovert, with a tendency to make bold statements in the clothes she wore, as well as changing her hairstyle and color frequently. Walt was a man of few words, but when he spoke, his comments reflected a keen intellect. He was long and lanky and in contrast to his wife had always kept his hair in a crew cut over the years even when it was not fashionable.

I copied the NTSB report on my fax machine so I could show it to Walt.

I was just ready to call it a day when the phone rang. Michelle was on the line.

She stated, "I have it!"

My thoughts had been elsewhere, and I asked in confusion, "You have what?"

"The man's name! I remembered it! It's Robert Perdue."

I exclaimed, "That's great! Did it just pop into your memory?"

"Actually, I had a little help. Ever since you told me about your investigation, I've been absent-minded at times, dwelling in the past. Anyhow, this afternoon I was between classes, sitting on a campus bench. I had planned to study but found myself pondering on the events of four years ago instead. A student joined me and said, 'Are you all right? You look lost.' When she said the word 'lost,' it hit me. The man's name was Perdue!"

"Oh, of course," I said, "*perdu* is French for 'lost.' Good job, Michelle!"

Then I stated, "Now all I have to do is find this Robert Perdue." And I added, "Were you under the impression that Perdue was a business acquaintance of your father's, or did you think they knew each other socially?"

"I have no idea."

"No matter. I'm grateful for your find."

As soon as I had replaced the receiver, I searched all the Southern California phone directories for a Robert Perdue. It proved a fruitless quest. A few Perdues were listed, but they all had different first names. Then I made some calls, equally unsuccessful.

I wrote down, "Robert Perdue?" on a piece of paper, slipped it into the file, and left my office.

Chapter 26

Peggy greeted me with, "Where have you been, Regula?" And she added, "Your raccoon tan, together with a white neck and arms, is a dead give-a-way!"

"Yes, you guessed right. Peter and I just got back from North Shore Tahoe. I'm trying to adjust to the 80's temperature we're experiencing down here," I said.

I was wearing a sundress, and glancing at my pale upper arms, I realized that they must indeed look comical in contrast to my tanned face.

She stated, "I'm just jealous!" Then she informed me, "Walt is in the workshop."

As I followed her down the hall, I said, "I hate to barge in on him."

"Don't be silly, he's just nursing his hobby!"

Opening the door to Walt's sanctuary, Peggy announced, "I'll leave you two alone and fix us some appetizers," and she headed back towards the kitchen.

I knew that the den had been converted into a workshop; nevertheless, I was astounded on entering. Kites of all shapes and sizes adorned three walls and were also stacked on shelves throughout the room. I was looking at an array of motifs in brilliant designs and colors. Along the fourth wall stretched a large workbench, covering about half the length of the good-sized room.

Next to the bench stood a rectangular open cabinet, holding materials such as plastic, fabric and crepe paper in a variety of colors, wooden dowels, bamboo skewers, balloon sticks, metal rods, rolls of twisted nylon line and wire. On top of the furniture tools were arranged, as well as sewing thread, felt tip pens and tape.

Walt stood over the workbench with his back to me, obviously making a kite.

Not sure whether he had heard me enter, I cleared my throat and said, "Hi, Walt! I don't mean to interrupt your work."

Turning around, he said, "Oh, hi, Regula! This is not work, but pure pleasure." And he added, "I'm almost done. Give me a few more minutes, and I'll be all yours."

"Do you mind if I watch?"

"Not at all."

Looking around the room once more, I commented, "Peggy told me that you've picked making kites as a hobby, but I had no idea you were such an artist!"

"Oh, I wouldn't go as far as calling myself an artist."

"Explain all the different shapes to me."

Pointing some of them out, he said, "The yellow one over there is a sled kite. The one next to it is a box kite. Below is a diamond, which is obviously the simplest design. If you look to your right, you'll see a delta. The red, blue and white at the very top of the far wall is a winged box."

"Of course," I said, "it looks like a box with wings attached." And I commented, "I like the one shaped like a bird the best. What is that form called?"

He grinned and said, "I have no idea, but I just call it a bird!"

The kite he was working on was smaller than most others I had admired in the room. It was diamond shaped and had a green-gold striped lizard drawn on a light purple background.

Pointing at it, I said, "This is cute. It's almost finished, right?"

"Yes. I'm just about done. My grandson is turning four next week, and I think he's ready for his first kite!"

"How exciting!" Then I asked, "What have you done to the kite so far? Please instruct me about the process."

He stated, "First I made a cardboard diamond template of 15" x 15" with a cross spar three inches from the top. Then I taped the purple sheet of plastic to my workbench. Using my template I marked the four corners and the spar cross point on the plastic sheet. Then I cut out the sail and also made a small hole at the spar cross point for the bridle. I drew the lizard onto the sail and colored it with felt tip markers.

"For the cross spar dihedral I used a two-inch plastic tube and inserted two bamboo skewers into both ends of the tube until they met in the center. This was to form the horizontal spar of the kite. For the kite's spine, I took two bamboo skewers and taped them together using masking tape. Then I wired the plastic dihedral to the center of one of the skewers. At that point I taped the spine to the kite sail and then did the same with the cross skewers."

He smiled and said, "Then you showed up."

I asked, "What's a dihedral?"

"A term used with aircraft wings. Might be too technical to explain to you."

I shrugged. Then I wanted to know, "So what's left to do?"

"Just attaching the tail and tying the flying line to the cross spars."

He walked over to the cabinet and pointed to rolls of fluorescent surveyors tape, asking me, "Your choice; which color for the tail?"

"Can you attach more than one?"

"Sure."

"Okay. Red and gold."

"Red and gold it is," he said, and he cut off about three yards each of the plastic streamers and looped them around the spine spar. He then measured 15 yards of nylon line, cut it, and tied it to the cross spars. He tied the other end to a small piece of cardboard tube, forming a handle for his grandson to hold onto.

"Done," Walt said.

I exclaimed, "I'm impressed!" And I added, "I bet you can't wait to go try it out with your grandson."

"Of course! I'll teach him the basics of aerodynamics. Like airplanes, kites are heavier than air and rely on aerodynamic forces to fly. Gas balloons, on the other hand, are lighter than air and depend on buoyancy forces to move." And he added, "Speaking of aircraft, what exactly did you want to know about planes?"

"I hope you won't mind answering a few questions, but can we sit someplace?" And pointing to my feet I explained, "I'm wearing these high-heeled sandals for the first time, and they are killing me."

"Sure," he said, "let's go up front to sit."

Peggy had set up some tortilla chips and salsa, as well as a platter of carrot and celery sticks on the bar counter dividing kitchen and dining room.

She was about to pour drinks when I said, "Not for me, thanks."

"I thought you liked Smirnoff?"

"I do, but I have to drive home."

"Come now, Regula; you only live eight blocks away."

"I could do a lot of harm in those blocks," I stated.

She rolled her eyes. Then she commented, "It's about time you showed up for some nibbles. Are you done with the interview?"

I sheepishly replied, "Actually, we haven't started yet."

Surprised, she looked at us and asked, "What on earth have you two been doing all this time?"

"I got instructed on how to make a kite," I replied.

While setting a Perrier in front of me she said, "Well, don't go flying it; that might take the better part of a week!" Then getting serious, she added, "Go ahead with your questions for Walt. I promise I won't interfere."

We made ourselves comfortable on the barstools, and then I addressed Walt, "I'm looking into an airplane crash resulting in two fatalities. According to the investigation of the National Transportation Safety Board, the crash was treated as an accident. I was recently hired to assess if foul play could have been a possibility."

I reached into my purse, took out the copy of the NTSB report, and handed it over.

Walt studied it at length and then stated, "This crash took place four years ago!"

I nodded.

He said, "There was no question of murder having been committed at the time?"

"No."

"What makes the people who hired you think so now, all of a sudden?"

"It's a long, complicated story, but I believe there is reason to look into it," I replied.

Peggy, forgetting her earlier resolution of not interfering, said, "In other words, you don't want to tell us, Regula!"

"That's right!" I said and smiled at her.

Turning back to Walt, I continued, "I'm coming to you for suggestions on how that plane could have been tampered with."

He surveyed the NTSB report once more and observed,

"The cause of the crash was inconclusive. Might have been due to mechanical failure, or the pilot could have suddenly taken ill."

After a pause, he asked, "Are you thinking someone slipped the pilot something that would cause him to lose consciousness?"

I thought about this suggestion and then said, "Judging from what I've learned so far in my investigation, I doubt that. Besides, that would be impossible to prove after a lapse of four years. I was thinking more along the line of 'Could have been caused by mechanical failure,' in the report."

Walt stated, "I don't follow you. Mechanical failure does not indicate any kind of 'tampering,' as you call it. Explosives are out of the question. The officials of the NTSB would have detected anything of that sort."

I said, "What I mean is, could any kind of sabotage to the aircraft have taken place and be made to look like mechanical failure?"

"Oh, I get you now." Then he continued, "I don't think that could have been the case since every pilot checks his plane out for possible vital defects before take-off."

Disappointed, I asked, "So you can't give me any hints at all?"

After a long pause, he said, "The only thing I can suggest might be fuel contamination."

"What would that involve?"

"A liquid would be added to the fuel, or possibly the fuel could be entirely replaced by such a liquid."

"You mean someone could have let the fuel out of the tank and substituted another liquid?"

Walt said, "Possibly. If it were added to the existing fuel, it would have to be clear in color. If replaced, it would have to be light blue."

"Meaning the fuel is normally blue?" I said.

"For a plane like the Cessna 152, it would be blue."

"Explain that to me a little better, please."

"Surely. The Cessna 152 fuel capacity is 26 gallons in two 13-gallon tanks. 100 low-lead fuel is used in this type of plane and has a blue tint to it. After taking a sample from the lowest point in the fuel system, the pilot holds the sample up to something white to check if the color is blue."

I asked, "How could the plane still take off and fly with a contaminant liquid added or substituted?"

He replied, "If I were going to sabotage a fuel system, I would drain the fuel down enough to get the plane into the air. Then I would fill the remainder of the tank with a dyed contaminant lighter than gasoline so it would stay on top. There would be just enough good fuel still in the lines for the plane to get into the air and then the contaminant finally would get to the engine, causing it to lose power, stall, and then crash."

"Could water be added?"

"Water wouldn't do. It's heavier than gasoline and would displace the fuel, and the pilot would drain water from the fuel tanks as a matter of routine. Also, the engine would never start."

"So what would you use?"

"Something lighter than gasoline that would not run in an engine and would burn in a fire or evaporate in a crash."

After thinking this information over, I stated, "So if the pilot checked his fuel before take-off, it would look all right to him."

"Exactly."

"And since the plane caught fire, it's almost a certainty that the tanks would not be found intact by the NTSB."

"I would think so," he answered.

I beamed at him, saying, "Well, Walt, you certainly gave me food for thought. Thank you very much."

Then I addressed Peggy. "You've been extremely patient. Thanks for the appetizers. Your salsa is superb! And now I had best head home and feed Peter."

I got up, hugged Peggy good-bye, waved to Walt and made my way out.

Chapter 27

When I returned from the gym the next morning, I found Peter on our back porch settled into his favorite lounge chair, reading the *LA Times*. I poured each of us a glass of lemonade and joined him.

Looking up from the paper, he inquired, "So how's your sleuthing coming along? Are you making progress?"

"Yes and no," I said.

"Tell me about the 'yes' first."

"I have a name to go with Steven Lamont's mystery acquaintance." And I told him what I'd learned from Michelle.

He said, "Robert Perdue. Not a common last name. He shouldn't be hard to find."

"Exactly what I thought, but so far my search has proved unproductive. If he lives in Southern California, his number is unlisted; I checked all the phone books. I called Thomas Teleford and Rachael Moreley, hoping they would know if Perdue had been a business acquaintance of Lamont. Neither one could recall the name Robert Perdue. I also reached the Prescott and Sosna families, as well as Teresa Cesar. None of them knew anyone by that name. When I talked to Scott, he remembered seeing a man saying good-bye to his dad and sister just as he was walking towards them at the end of the skiing day. So that at least confirms Michelle's story."

Then I said, more to myself than to Peter, "I have got to find that man. I am convinced the whole mystery revolves around what Lamont learned from Perdue. I am certain the angry words Michelle overheard her father shout at someone were in reaction to whatever he had gleaned from that man."

He nodded understandingly and said, "I know you're frustrated at this point, but you'll find him. Look at how hard it seemed to locate Shelby, and she would have actually been in close reach from the beginning!"

Smiling, I stated, "You always know how to cheer me up!" Then I continued, "Peggy and Walt said 'Hello' to you."

"You ran into them?"

"Not exactly," I replied. "I went to pay them a visit," and I told him all about it.

He laughed. "I knew, of course, that Walt took up making kites ever since he semi-retired, but you make it sound like these kites are extraordinary creations!"

"Oh, they are! Some of them are magnificent. You'll have to view them yourself one day."

Then, getting serious, he stated, "So Walt came up with fuel contamination. Yes, that makes sense." And looking at me searchingly, he added, "I get the feeling you're disappointed with that solution?"

"Well," I reflected, "it would be easier to eliminate suspects if there was any mechanical knowledge involved, but simply adding or substituting a liquid to the tank seems like child's play."

"I see what you mean. But surely you can eliminate a few suspects from the simple standpoint of them having been physically unable to get to that airport."

"Whom do you suggest I cross off the suspect list?"

"The young people without access to a car, for instance."

I stated, "I thought about all that and came to the conclusion that everyone would've had access to transportation."

"Really?"

"You see, each family kept a four-wheel-drive at Lake Tahoe, and the ones that were too young to drive could have easily taken a shuttle bus to the Truckee airport that night or early the next morning."

And I continued, "As far as the people not vacationing at Lake Tahoe were concerned, they could have taken a commercial flight to Reno, driven to Truckee by rental car or taxi, and returned on an early morning flight back to Los Angeles. I admit, in Rachael Moreley's case that would've taken some real hustling in order for her to be at her desk at nine that morning to answer Lamont's call."

He commented, "At least you can safely disregard Michelle as a suspect at this point."

"Why?"

"She's paying your fee now!"

"That could be a clever disguise," I prompted.

He threw up his hands, exclaiming, "There isn't a soul you trust!"

"Wrong. I trust you!"

We sat in silence for a while, and then I asked, "How about that trip to Central Mexico you suggested?"

Perplexed he said, *"I suggested?"* Then he burst out laughing and asked, "For how long?"

"Oh, maybe a week or so," I answered. And getting to my feet, I said, "Be right back."

Moments later I joined him again, and unfolding a map, I said, "I'll show you what *you* had in mind!"

Looking at the proposed itinerary, Peter remarked, "This will take longer than a week."

"But it will be great fun!" I replied.

Chapter 28

While cruising twenty thousand feet above the Pacific on a Mexicana flight to Guadalajara on Friday, April 2, my thoughts regressed to the previous two days. Overjoyed with Peter agreeing to venture into a Central Mexican vacation, I had jumped into action of planning the trip. The idea was to rent a car in Guadalajara and first travel north, then east as far as San Miguel de Allende. The journey would then take us south to Pátzcuaro, followed by turning west to the Lake Chapala area and finally ending back at Guadalajara; -- in other words, going in a full circle. James Bradley lived in a town called Ajijic near Lake Chapala, so we planned to pay him a visit towards the end of the trip.

I had informed Scott and Michelle of our plans. Michelle had proposed to pay part of the expenses, but I declined her offer; after all, this was basically a vacation.

The evening before our departure, I had called our kids to notify them of our forthcoming trip. I smiled to myself at the recollection. Typically, our son just said, "Central Mexico; good choice. Have a wonderful time!" Our daughter, on the other hand, reacted to the news in her "Sunshine" fashion, as Peter would put it. She exclaimed, "What? Another trip? You just came back from Tahoe!" When told the approximate itinerary, she warned, "Be careful what you eat and drink. No tap water. Don't even brush your teeth with it. Make sure you never drive once it gets dark. You don't want to be ambushed by *banditos*! And Mom, leave your jewelry at home."

I glanced at Peter reclining in his seat, seemingly asleep.

He blinked and said, "Are you wearing your nicotine patch?"

"I forgot," I said, with a tinge of guilt. "It's only a three-hour flight. I'll survive."

Then he asked, "So where did you make hotel reservations?"

"Just in Guadalajara for our accommodations the first night and the couple of nights at the end of the journey. I reserved the rental car at the airport for tomorrow morning. We can take a taxi to the hotel. I thought we should play the rest of our trip by ear. That way, we won't be tied to any particular place and date."

"An *ad libitum* adventure!"

"Well put!"

Then he inquired, "Did you call the accountant guy?"

"Not yet," I replied. "When we get to his town, I'll make that call. I'll explain that we are on vacation and would like to stop by. I know I'm taking a chance that he might not be home."

"What's your reason for not letting him know ahead of time?"

"A surprise visit has the advantage that he won't prepare the answers to my questions in advance."

Astonished, Peter said, "Is he your prime suspect, then?"

"Let's just say one of the suspects," I answered.

"Did you pack your gun?"

"Well, I wasn't sure what the gun laws are with respect to international travel, so I left my pistol at home. I probably couldn't make a citizen's arrest in Mexico anyhow." And I added, "Even if James Bradley turns out to be our villain, I doubt he would feel threatened at this point. After all, we'll just pay him a friendly visit and ask some questions."

Peter nodded, and then closed his eyes again.

Chapter 29

The cab driver dropped us in front of Hotel Fenix in downtown Guadalajara at 5:30 p.m. After checking in and a quick freshening up, we started our exploration of the city on foot.

Guadalajara has a large population of 4,000,000 and is at an elevation of over five thousand feet. We took a long walk into the historic part of town. The cobblestoned streets led in and out of beautifully landscaped square plazas. In between squares we strode along orange orchards and fountains, flanked by shops, markets, and restaurants. Goods, as well as horse-drawn carriage rides, were offered along the promenade. Cars were off limits in most streets in the *Centro Historico* district, the whole area being pedestrian-friendly.

The buildings' architecture had a definite colonial influence. I could easily imagine we were strolling along in a town in Italy or Spain. One of the most beautiful buildings was the *Teatro Degollado*, which stood behind the flowing waters of a fountain. The Cathedral of Guadalajara with its tiled steeples was the center of the district. Peter and I were not the only ones out for a stroll; the streets were full of folks enjoying the evening. We noticed few tourists, however.

That evening, Peter kissed me goodnight and stated, "I'm looking forward to venturing into this part of Mexico. It'll be a totally new experience." And he added, "You didn't give me much time to brush up on my Spanish, though!"

"I'm sure the language is the same one they speak in Cancun!" I chuckled, and turned off the light.

Chapter 30

Saturday morning we took another cab back to the airport to pick up the rental car. This proved not to be the simple task we had expected. They first tried to equip us with a standard transmission vehicle. It took some wheeling and dealing on our part, but we finally were handed the keys to the midsize automatic transmission car I had been guaranteed when making the reservation. Trying to locate it was another adventure. The woman at the rental desk had given us wrong directions to where we would find the car parked. We tracked back and forth in the parking lot hauling our luggage. We asked several people where to find the rental car parking spaces, but no one knew. Finally a boy about twelve years old helped us with the luggage and found the people that could guide us in the right direction. It took three more persons!

Peter smiled and said, "Isn't it wonderful that no one seems to be in a hurry?"

I shot him a look and said, "I'm not in *siesta* mode yet."

Eventually we took possession of the car and were merrily on our way out of town. When on unfamiliar ground the driving was usually left up to me, and Peter acted as navigator, having a natural aptitude for reading maps.

We headed northeast and then stopped at Lagos de Moreno for the night. Despite its name, we didn't discover any lakes. The following morning we traveled on, southeast bound.

Guanajuato with a population of 95,000 and breath-catching elevation of 6740 feet is one of the most beautiful

"Old World charm" places we had ever come across. Once we found our way in, that was! We knew beforehand that car traffic in the *Centro* was limited and mostly underground, reserving the town to pedestrians. We had also been informed that to access the hotels downtown, one had to drive into a tunnel. Finding this tunnel was another matter. We had already driven around what we thought was the correct area twice, had made several U-turns on the narrow streets with oncoming traffic, when we finally gave in to hiring a guide. A "guide" meant one of the young men standing on every street corner waving cars down. We finally stopped, holding up traffic, while the young man explained that the only way you could find the entrance to the tunnel, and consequently a hotel, was to have him climb into your car and lead the way. Our guide was Miguel, and I must say, without him we would still be looking for the tunnel! Miguel took us on a long and adventurous journey through narrow tunnels with cars parked along the sides. We came up for air twice, and our young guide jumped out and back into the car in front of hotels, shaking his head -- "No vacancy,"-- and down into the tunnels we went again. Miguel came back from the third hotel with a big grin, meaning he had found an accommodation for us.

We had time in the late afternoon to explore the town. The way the city had been built some 300 years ago was magnificent. The streets were cobblestoned, which was a little hard on the feet but lovely to look at. Peter informed me that the streets and sidewalks were actually not cobblestone since they were square, not round, but lacking a better word, I would still call them "cobbled." The buildings and churches were architectural masterpieces, in my opinion. We visited lots of churches, the most famous of which was the Cathedral Basilica of Guanajuato.

After dinner, as we strolled around town enjoying the street performers and Mariachi bands playing everywhere, I exclaimed, "I just love it here! I'm so glad we decided to stay two days."

The following morning we took a taxi to the *Museo de los Momias*. The museum was crowded, so there were other folks interested in viewing ancient corpses! In spite of the morbid environment, I found the subjects fascinating and educational. Apparently there is something in the soil that naturally delays decay, so the bodies buried about a hundred years ago looked remarkably well preserved. Some of them were rather unpleasant to look at. All we could do was return their stares!

Back in town we took the funicular up to the monument of *El Pipila*, which sits high above the city. From up there we had the most spectacular view of the comely town surrounded by mountains. Peter took umpteen pictures. We even spotted our hotel, and he mounted his telephoto lens and zoomed in on it. We felt gratified to have come by funicular. Even though we were both in good condition, we could feel the high altitude when hiking uphill or, even worse, climbing the 58 steps up to our hotel room!

In the early evening we visited the inside of the Basilica of our Lady of Guanajuato. The ornate altar was decorated with the most gorgeous flower arrangements of gold, blue and white. From the ceiling hung chandeliers, sparkling like diamonds.

Chapter 31

Early the next day we headed east, driving through a mountain area. The dense frost covering trees and ground gave the illusion of being surrounded by snow. For about fifteen miles we drove in heavy fog. Luckily there was little traffic, so I could drive as slowly as I pleased. Riding down the back side of the mountain, an attractive small city of about 41,000 inhabitants called Dolores Hidalgo came into view. It was time for a short restroom stop. We found parking close to *El Centro*, and I went in search of a bathroom. After unsuccessfully hunting for what seemed like hours, I located the *Oficina de Turismo* and asked directions to *cuartos de baño públicos*. Once found, I handed the obligatory two *pesos* to the attendant to receive a tiny wad of toilet paper.

Churches were by far the most impressive buildings in every town, and the one at the center of this town square was no exception. It boasted a most magnificent gilded side altar.

On the road between Dolores Hidalgo and San Miguel de Allende, we had to stop twice because cows decided to cross the street. We arrived in San Miguel around four o'clock that afternoon and found lodging smack in the very center of town.

Taking a before-dinner stroll, I commented, "What a charming little place!"

Peter said, "Yes, but it's freezing!"

We were now at an altitude of over six thousand feet, and even having donned our heavy jackets we felt chilled. We noticed that the place was full of Americans and

Canadians, not necessarily tourists, but people that lived there.

We dined at a Cajun restaurant, which served excellent Jambalaya. On our walk back to the hotel we stopped for after-dinner drinks of margaritas.

Thunder and lightning woke me up in the middle of the night. The volume of thunder was tremendous, since we were high up, surrounded by mountains. Heavy rain pounded against the window shutters of our balcony.

Peter murmured, "This isn't supposed to be the rainy season yet," and promptly went back to sleep.

Early the next morning, as the rain came down in buckets, he stated, "Let's get out of here. It is too cold, too wet, and full of *Gringos!*"

Amused I said, "What do you think *we* are?"

We had a pleasant four-and-a-half-hour drive south to Morelia. The landscape was hilly and we passed a couple of lakes, one of them almost dried up. We drove along vast agricultural fields but could not determine what type of crops was growing. We spotted goats, mules and horses next to the highway.

Driving into the City of Morelia was a hectic experience. Traffic was heavy and congested in this city with a population of about 710,000. Although still at a very high altitude, we were delighted to find sunshine and warmer temperatures. By pure luck we found the *Centro* and the hotel I had looked up on the Internet. Best Western Hotel Casino was located at center town, across from the cathedral. Hotel Casino, to our disappointment, was not a gambling establishment, as the name implied.

The inner city of Morelia was beautiful, especially at night with its highlighted churches and wrought iron street lamps all along the boulevards. On our first evening we ended up at the *Centro Historico* about fifteen blocks from our hotel. We strolled in and out of numerous little parks adorned with exquisite fountains all lit up. We felt the town was safe to walk around after dark; we just had to watch out we didn't get run over by cars. Traffic at night was still hectic and congested. When vehicles got stuck at an intersection, there was a tremendous amount of honking horns. Pedestrians had to fight their way across the street at each block.

We explored a good portion of the city in the two days we stayed in Morelia. It would have taken us a week to see everything worth seeing. On our last night in the town, I stepped out on the hotel room balcony around midnight and found traffic still heavy on the street below.

I exclaimed, "Where are all these people going? Don't they ever sleep in this place?"

Chapter 32

On Friday we drove westward and arrived in Pátzcuaro, a European looking, picturesque village. It reminded us of small towns in Italy with its archways and sidewalk restaurants. There was an outdoor *Mercado* as in all other places we had seen. Exploring the center town area, we came upon two large plazas. The first boasted a statue of a woman martyr in its center, the other a huge fountain. We sat on a bench near the fountain and watched as some boys tried to retrieve a hat, which apparently one of them had dropped into the water. The endeavor was comical to observe. They first tried to make waves with their hands to get the hat to float closer to the edge, which proved unsuccessful. One youngster disappeared and came back with a broom and then tried to make bigger waves. The hat floated even farther away. Eventually one kid jumped into the ice-cold water and finally fetched the sombrero out of the fountain. Peter and I both clapped, applauding the happy ending.

We were now at an altitude of over 7000 feet, and even though warm and pleasant in the afternoon, it was freezing as soon as the sun went down. There wasn't much nightlife, so we turned in early, after a little stroll to digest our dinner.

The following day we took a taxi to Lago de Pátzcuaro and ventured on a 20-minute boat ride to the Isla de Janitzio. The island was a hill and looked marvelous from a distance as well as up close. The houses were mostly painted white or light colors. Naturally, a church had been built even on such a small island. At the very top of the hill stood a commanding, approximately 130-foot statue of *Don José María Morelos y Pavón*. We walked up to the monument, a steep hike on mostly cobblestones. I was wearing sandals and wished I had changed into tennis shoes. Once on top, Peter decided to climb up inside the hollow statue all the way to the outstretched arm. I passed -- too claustrophobic for me. I went in search of a restroom instead, and little Indian girls followed me around begging for *pesos*.

As we came back to Patzcuaro in the early evening, Peter said, "Tomorrow is Easter and we'll be on the road; let's find a church that offers a Saturday evening Mass."

We found one on top of a little hill and, since folks were flocking towards it, we were pretty sure there was going to be a Mass. We settled into a pew. The church was already decorated for Easter festivities with white flowing banners and yellow-and-white tulips. Above the altar there was an exquisite statue of the Madonna, dressed in blue, flared robes.

The priest gave a lengthy and animated sermon, gesticulating with his arms to make a point. I concentrated on his rapid Spanish for a while, only able to understand a few words here and there. Soon the effort got too strenuous, and my mind started to wander. I was dwelling on the Easter egg hunt I would miss with my grandchildren. I even got a little misty-eyed. Grandchildren will do that to you!

As we got to the part in the Mass where the congregation 'passes the peace,' the tiny lady in the pew ahead of us turned around. She must have been at least 100 years old. Her weathered face showed deep laugh-lines around mouth and eyes. When she looked into my eyes, I read ageless wisdom in hers.

She took my hand into the palms of both of hers, and, never wavering her sincere glance, said, *"La paz del señor esté con usted"* – The peace of the Lord be with you.

I was touched. Peter was an undemonstrative "peace passer" at church as a rule. However, as the old lady extended her peace greeting to him, I sensed that he too felt honored by her sincerity.

On Easter Sunday, April 11, we made it to Lake Chapala in six hours. We first stopped in the town of Chapala. The lake had receded so much that one couldn't honestly claim the town lay by the lake. We were happy to perceive a pleasantly warm temperature in the low 80's. A short 10-kilometer drive took us to Ajijic.

We found an excellent hotel right by the lake. Our room was a suite and sported a large balcony with a lake view. After checking in, we strolled down to the water, where people were horseback riding along the shore. We spotted Delta-gliders taking off from the mountaintops above the town. The locals drove their cars through dirt and grass right down to the water. We presumed lots of folks from Guadalajara had fled the city to spend Easter Sunday at Lake Chapala.

When we turned in that night, Peter said, "So tomorrow you start working?"

"Yep. And you too!" I replied, and grinned at him.

Chapter 33

Making sure I would not disturb him too early, I waited until 10:30 the following morning before I made my call to James Bradley. He sounded congenial and gave me directions to his residence.

On our way there in the afternoon, Peter asked, "How far is it, and at what time are we expected?"

I replied, "It's only about a mile and a half farther down along the lake. Bradley said we could drop by anytime we wish."

"Tell me, Regula, what exactly is my job during this interview?"

"Oh nothing earthshaking! Just ask questions that pop into your head, and keep your eyes and ears open."

"I can manage that," he retorted.

The driveway leading to Bradley's house was laid with brownish-red painted paving stones, which complemented the red tile roof, stark white stucco and turquoise framed windows of the sizeable home. Rounded arches adorned the front porch and door.

We climbed out of the car and approached the entrance. As if on cue, a middle-aged woman opened the door.

She said, "*Señor y señora Huber?*"

"*Si.*"

"*Vengan, por favor,*" she begged, and led us to the side of the house through an arched opening in the stucco wing wall, which created a gracious entryway to the backyard. We followed her past a patio flanked by an oval-shaped pool. Then she led us on a pathway edged by shrubs and bushes. As we turned the corner, I stood in awe at the picture proffered in front of us. We had arrived at the *Garden of Eden*, it seemed! There were orchids of various shapes and sizes in an array of reds, purples, yellows, greens, pinks and white arranged around a small cascading water fountain.

I exclaimed, "How absolutely lovely!"

Peter, obviously equally impressed, said, "I've never seen so many exotic flowers all in one place!"

In the midst of this splendor, a man clad in shorts, a t-shirt and a wide-rimmed straw hat was bending over a potted plant with blooming yellow flowers.

Pointing in his direction, the woman said in broken English, "Mr. Bradley, he is there," and she turned around and walked back to the house.

Bradley straightened himself up and then looked at us. He said, "Hello, folks. Welcome to Ajijic!" Then his gaze rested on me. He scrutinized me from head to toe.

Chuckling, he exclaimed, "*You're* R.A. Huber? Well, I'll be darned!"

Bemused, I said, "What did you expect?"

"Oh, I don't know. Big and tough looking, I guess." And surveying me again, he added, "Certainly not as well turned out and genteel."

Smiling, I said, "Thanks for the compliment." Then I commented, "You're growing the most gorgeous orchids!"

"Yes," he said. "You've caught me tending to my hobby."

As he started to take off his rubber gloves, I quickly said, "Please don't interrupt what you're doing. We'd love to watch."

"All right. I'll finish, then. I just have a couple more to re-pot."

He squeezed the pot from side to side, loosening the mix until he could easily remove the pot from the plant.

Then he cleaned the old mix off the plant and removed the dead roots with clippers.

Proceeding to divide the plant in half, he said, "I have to make sure I leave at least three root-parts on each plant." Then he put each section into two individual pots, surrounding the roots with fresh mix. He carefully added the mixture by rotating the pots and distributing the new mixture to about one inch below the rim.

As he did this, he explained, "I need to make sure the pseudo-bulbs are only partially buried."

I asked, "What kind of a potting mix do you use?"

"I use a mixture of fir bark and horticultural charcoal. I soak the bark for 24 hours before I mix it with the charcoal."

Then he lined up an assortment of plants, obviously already divided and re-potted before our arrival, and watered them all thoroughly, saying, "These won't need watering for the next two weeks."

And finally removing his rubber gloves, he stated, "Okay. Done. I'm all yours now!"

Enthusiastically, I said, "Do you mind sharing some of your secrets about growing these horticultural wonders?"

He looked at Peter and said, "I don't want to bore anyone."

Peter stated, "Not at all! I'm interested. I write, and I might introduce orchids in my next book."

Bradley said, "All right. What do you folks want to know?" And he added, "Or I should rather ask, what do you already know about orchids?"

"Nothing, except that they are gorgeous to look at, and I assume it takes great pains to grow them," I said.

"They are really not all that hard to take care of. You just need to give them what they like." And pointing at the plants he had just watered, he continued, "Take these *Cymbidiums*, for instance. They are just about as easy to grow as geraniums, as long as you provide the climate they need and feed and water them generously. They like the morning and afternoon sun."

Peter asked, "What fertilizer do you use?"

"There are several orchid fertilizers on the market. I like to use the kind with a good percentage of nitrogen, phosphorous and potassium content, as well as some copper, iron and zinc." And he added, "Orchids are frugal plants; they like to be fed regularly, but in small dosage."

"Is the climate in this region ideal for orchids?" I asked.

"Yes, for some of them," he replied. "The Lake Chapala area has a semitropical climate. The lake, combined with the high altitude, gives this region a pleasantly warm temperature all year 'round. The highs are between 75 and 86 degrees and the lows between 46 and 60. The plants like the humidity coming from the lake as well."

Walking around the fountain, I pointed at an approximately eight-inch plant that carried about five exquisite fuchsia and light-pink flowers per stem, asking, "What is this one called?"

"That's a *Cattleya*. The exact name of this particular *Cattleya* is *Hwa Yuan Bay 'She Shu'.*"

"That's a mouthful," Peter commented.

Mr. Bradley pointed out, "The yellow plant right next to it is also a *Cattleya*, named *Luna Jaune.*"

We came upon an area with big, tall bushes to one side, and Bradley explained, "In this section I mostly keep *Paphiopedilums*. They grow one flower per stem for the most part. They like shady conditions and soft, filtered light. They need to be kept moist." And pointing at an orchid boasting a bright red flower, he added, "My favorite! This *Paphiopedilum* is called '*Living Fire.*'"

We strolled to another part of the orchid garden, and I exclaimed, "What a magnificent array of colors!"

Our host stated, "All these are *Oncidiums*."

The tag inserted in one of the pots read: "*Oncidium, Sharry Baby*."

He said, "Smell the fragrance!"

I bent down to the dark-red flowers and, surprised, stated, "Smells like chocolate!"

Leading us yet to another section of vegetation, Bradley, clearly enjoying his role as a 'tour-guide,' pointed out, "Over here are *Dendrobiums*."

I took a particular fancy to a plant with strongly-scented bright lavender flowers growing on upright stems, looking like canes. There was a velvety texture to these orchids.

The tag read, '*Sweet Fragrance*,' and I commented, "How appropriate!"

Then we came to an area cordoned off with a sign: *Species*.

Bradley pointed to a plant with white flowers and said, "This is the national flower of Brazil, named *purpurata var carnea*, better known as '*Lady Godiva*.' He continued, "And the yellow orchid supported by the trellis next to it is *Vanilla planifolia*. You heard correctly. Vanilla is an orchid. It is indigenous to Mexico and may have been used up to 1,000 years ago by the Totonac tribe as a flavoring."

"What do you grow in there?" I asked, pointing at a small structure a little distance away.

He stated, "The greenhouse is relatively new; I added it a few months ago. I keep some of the fussier orchid types in there. At the moment I grow mostly *Phalaenopsis* in the greenhouse, but during the rainy season I'll transfer some of the other plants as well. Orchids like moisture, but they hate to be soaked."

Peter said, "The rainy season is in summer, correct?"

"Uh-huh, from early July to late September."

As we entered the greenhouse I felt the strong humidity surrounding us. I imagined that this might be what the air felt like in a tropical rainforest. At a glance, the greenhouse looked sparsely stocked. Purple, orange, red, white, yellow and green orchids were bunched together on three rows of shelves. One among them particularly caught my eye. Its flowers were delicately striped purple and light yellow. The nametag attached read, *Phalaenopsis, Sogo Maria 'Oriental Stripes.'* The rest of the space in the greenhouse was virtually empty.

I said, "Until the rainy season these plants have the greenhouse all to themselves. Is there a reason to keep them so close together?"

"Believe it or not, they like each others' company. One should never isolate orchids."

Then Peter asked, "So these are all Phala – something's?"

"Correct. Most of them are *Phalaenopsis*, except that funny-looking green species on the top shelf. That's a species called *philippinense var album*. That particular species did not do well for me outside, so now that I brought it in here, it seems to recuperate."

Then Peter inquired, "I see that these pots stand on some fancy trays. Why is that?"

Bradley explained, "Those are humidity trays. They're plastic trays with a grid. You fill the trays with water and place the plants on the grid. As I mentioned, orchids don't like soggy conditions at their roots."

Then I said, "I notice the two small room humidifiers and understand what they're for, but what is the purpose of the little fans next to them?"

"Those are for air circulation. Besides needing humidity of 50 to 70 percent, these plants also require a gentle air movement. Both humidifiers and fans must be placed about three to four feet away from the orchids."

As we left the greenhouse, I said, "Thank you for sharing your hobby with us." And I added, "Amazing what a big collection of orchids you amassed in just four years!"

He grinned. "It gets addictive after a while. Besides, orchids are like rabbits. They sort of multiply!"

"Yes, we watched you multiply the *Cymbidiums* earlier," I remarked.

"You paid attention!" he said, beaming.

Then he suggested, "And now let's have some refreshments and you can get to the point of your visit, Mrs. Huber," and he winked at me.

Chapter 34

While leading us back to the patio, Bradley commented, "You're lucky you found me at home. I just came back from dropping my wife off in San Diego last night."

Peter asked, "You drove all the way to San Diego?"

"No. I meant flying."

Puzzled, Peter said, "You mean you dropped your wife off at the Guadalajara airport?"

"No, we flew to San Diego in my own plane."

We made ourselves comfortable on the patio chairs. Bradley took off his hat, enabling me to study him more thoroughly. He sported a full head of white hair. There wasn't anything particularly remarkable about him. The gray eyes glancing at us from behind gold-rimmed glasses appeared intelligent.

He inquired how we liked our trip into Central Mexico. We elaborated on our impressions of the places we had visited, and told him the story of how we had failed to find the tunnel leading to the hotels in Guanajuato by ourselves.

He laughed. "I wouldn't be surprised if the entrance to the tunnels was designed in such a complicated way on purpose, so jobs could be created for the guides! All in all it sounds like you have enjoyed your journey so far."

"We've loved every minute of it," I said.

"What are your plans after you leave Ajijic?"

Peter answered, "We'll spend two more days in Guadalajara, and then our trip will come to an end, I'm afraid."

At that moment the middle-aged woman reappeared, and our host asked, "What would you like to drink? I can offer you beer, wine, margaritas, Coke, or we have freshly squeezed lemonade."

I said, "Lemonade sounds lovely," then, remembering my daughter's warning about drinking the water, "or maybe" --

Bradley smiled and said, "You don't have to worry, Mrs. Huber. We have a water purification system installed."

"Lemonade for me too, please," said Peter.

Our host turned to the woman and said, *"Por favor tráiganos tres limonades, Juanita."*

"Si, señor."

After she left, I asked, "Juanita is your housekeeper?"

"Yes, she is."

As soon as the refreshments were served, I felt it was time to get to the point and asked, "Why did you take early retirement?"

He replied, "The accounting at Lamont & Associates was being modernized with a new electronic system. Frankly, at the age of 62, I didn't want to learn the new system."

Peter said, "I can sympathize with that."

Then I commented, "I can see you're enjoying your retirement to the fullest. You have a beautiful home, an interesting and rewarding hobby, and you and your wife seem to be well taken care of by Juanita."

"Yes, we're lucky we can afford it. With my social security benefits, the pension from Lamont & Associates, our savings and investments over the years, and a modest inheritance my wife collected, we can do nicely here."

Peter put in, "What kind of aircraft do you own?"

"A Piper Arrow, single engine."

I asked, "Forgive my ignorance, but how many passengers does such a plane accommodate?"

"Four."

"Did you already fly before your retirement?"

He answered, "I took flying instructions just before I retired, but I didn't own a plane then. I purchased the Piper Arrow after we moved to Mexico."

"What got you interested in becoming a pilot?"

"Steven Lamont introduced me to it. He was so exuberant about flying so I decided to try it." And grinning, he added, "Now I'm hooked."

Peter inquired, "Is your wife vacationing in San Diego?"

"Not exactly. Her sister is recuperating from surgery. My wife went to help take care of her. I took her there on Friday and meant to stay with them over the Easter weekend, but by early Sunday morning I had the urge to get back." He added, "I don't do well around convalescent people and felt I was only in the way."

After a pause, I asked, "Mr. Bradley, does the name Robert Perdue mean anything to you?"

He took a couple of seconds to think, and then repeated, "Robert Perdue? It rings a bell, but I can't place it for the moment. Who is he?"

"I was hoping you could tell me," I replied.

He seemed to reflect, and then said, "Oh, I remember now. I never knew the man; I only saw his name on paper."

"At Lamont & Associates?"

"Yes."

"A client?"

He nodded.

"Whose client was he?" I asked.

"I don't know. Could've been Lamont's, Teleford's or any of the junior brokers'. I came across the name in my capacity as accountant; whose client he was did not interest me."

"You were only interested in figures, huh?"

"Correct."

I probed further, "Do you by any chance remember where Robert Perdue lived?"

"You've got to be kidding! Do you honestly think I would remember an address?"

I said, "Not really. Just a town would help."

After a pause, he stated, "I think Robert Perdue had an out-of-state address, possibly somewhere in Nevada. I can't be more specific than that. I'm not even sure if that's right."

We sat quietly for a while. Then I said, "Well, Mr. Bradley, you helped us a lot in our investigation."

He remarked, "I still can't get it into my head that the Lamonts could have been murdered."

As he said this, I perceived an odd look in his eyes. Did the look express sadness, or possibly fear?

Then he said, "Please keep me informed."

We thanked him kindly for his hospitality and got up to leave.

Chapter 35

On the drive back to our hotel, Peter teased, "So Bradley thinks you're *genteel!*"

"James Bradley is clearly a man of wisdom," I retorted.

Chuckling he said, "Your racquetball opponents would surely disagree."

"There are great benefits to the diversity of modern woman!"

Getting serious, I said, "So what did we learn from Bradley?"

"Other than that he has an impressive house with a pool, a fabulous orchid plantation, a maid and a plane?"

I remarked, "Did you get the feeling that Bradley was uncomfortable during the interview?"

"Not particularly. Are you experiencing women's intuition?"

"It's more than that."

"What's on your mind?"

"For instance, didn't it strike you as strange the way he justified his good fortune by itemizing his income?"

"Well, Regula, you dragged that out of him!"

"Oh, did I? I thought I was being diplomatic."

Then he said, "What's your point? Do you think Bradley embezzled money from Lamont & Associates?"

"It's a possibility." And I added, "I learned during the very first phone conversation with Bradley that he took early retirement. I already wondered back then what his reason was."

"So you don't believe his explanation of not wanting to get involved with a new accounting system at the age of 62? Sounds reasonable to me."

I said, "Yes, it does. But if he's the criminal, it would have conveniently given him a plausible reason for leaving."

After a pause, he said, "You made progress as far as the Perdue guy is concerned. Now you know he exists and possibly lives in the state of Nevada." He continued, "Whatever this Perdue told Lamont seems to be business related and not a private matter, since the fellow was a client."

"All I have to do is find him," I said.

Then he went on, "The fact that Bradley admitted he had come across the name would suggest that he's innocent."

"Not necessarily," I stated. "He had to assume that I already knew Perdue was a client, or could find out from someone else. So his admitting to having seen the name on paper only was actually clever, if he had something to hide."

As we pulled into the hotel parking lot, I muttered, "One thing is for sure. There are way too many pilots in this case!"

Chapter 36

We arrived home early in the evening on Thursday, April 15. Among numerous messages on our answering machine, there was one that puzzled me. It was from my office space landlord. He said to call as soon as I got back; he had an urgent message.

Peter said, "Do you have any idea what that could be about?"

"None," I replied. "I've paid the rent on time. I can't imagine what his urgency is about."

Then, looking at the time, I said, "It will have to wait until tomorrow. The landlord's offices are closed."

At nine o'clock the next morning, after tossing my first load of dirty laundry into the washer, I made the call. I was informed that my office in Pasadena had been broken into on Tuesday night, April 13. The lady occupying the office space next to mine had noticed the broken doorframe first thing Wednesday morning. She knew the break-in had to have occurred on the previous night. She came to her office daily and when she left at 5:00 p.m. on Tuesday, the doorframe was intact. The landlord had notified the police and was told they could not investigate until the renter was present. He gave me a number and a name to contact at the Police Department in case I wanted to file a report. Since I was expected back by Friday, the landlord had already hired door repair people and they would be there Friday afternoon. In the meantime a chain and padlock had been installed around the broken door.

I decided the dirty laundry from our trip would have to stay dirty a while longer. I made a quick stop at the landlord's office to pick up the padlock key, and then headed for Pasadena.

On my way over, I contemplated what the point of breaking into my office could be. The only valuable item I kept there was my Staunton Rosewood chess set. I was not thinking of its monetary worth, but rather of the sentimental value to me personally. The set had belonged to my late father, and I cherished the memory of playing chess with him on that particular set.

I undid the temporary lock, removed the chain and stood at the broken door surveying the damage for a brief moment, and then opened it. In shock, I stood there livid. My desk chair, as well as the client chair, was overturned, and the fax machine had been flung to the floor. My precious chess figures were scattered all over the room, obviously tossed around in a fury. As far as I could tell at a glance, nothing had been taken. There was just an overall mess.

I opened the top desk drawer and noticed the petty cash envelope was empty. I walked over to the file cabinet and took out the Lamont file. Nothing was missing from it.

With some dismay, I picked up the chess figures and checked each piece carefully before setting it back on its proper place on the chessboard. None were damaged, thank God. Then I resolutely put the rest of the room back in order.

That accomplished, I said to myself: Enough of feeling violated. Get to work, Regula!

Chapter 37

My first call was to a fellow private eye I knew in Las Vegas.

"Hello, Burt! R.A. Huber here."

"Well, hi there! How are you?"

"Good. I just came back from a trip to Central Mexico."

He asked, "Were you on vacation or sent there on a job?"

"A little of both," I replied.

Then I stated, "I'm afraid I only call you when I need a favor."

"Oh, you've helped me out a few times too. What can I do for you?"

"I need to find someone by the name of Robert Perdue. He lives in the state of Nevada, but I don't know in what town."

"Robert Perdue? How do you spell the last name?"

"I think P-e-r-d-u-e. But I'm not 100 percent sure."

Burt said, "I'll see what I can conjure up."

"Thanks a million," I said, and we hung up.

My next call was to Sgt. Wolf. I was lucky to catch him at his desk.

"Hello, R.A. Huber! Are you getting anywhere with your child-client case?"

"I've made some progress," I replied.

He laughed, "Leave it to you to dig up dirt from four years ago!"

I told him of my findings, ending with the recent trip to Mexico and the interview with James Bradley, being

careful not to mention any names. Then I informed him
of my office break-in.

He said, "Did you report it to the Pasadena police?"

"The landlord did. I was supposed to follow up on
it upon my return, but I'm not going to bother. Except
for some petty cash, amounting to twenty dollars at most,
nothing was taken."

"What do you make of the break-in?"

I replied, "I'm convinced the perpetrator wanted to
have a look at my current case file. Taking the little cash
and then throwing the furniture around was to make me
think the thief was angry he didn't find a better haul."

"I see. Was anything missing from your records?"

"My criminal is much too clever to have actually taken
anything from the file. It satisfied him to see how far I'd
progressed with the investigation."

"When did you see the accountant in Mexico?"

"Monday afternoon."

"I guess it's possible he could have boarded a flight
out of Guadalajara on Tuesday and could make it to your
office in Pasadena by that night."

I said, "He flies his own plane. He also knew I wasn't
due back in the U.S. until yesterday."

After a pause, the sergeant said, "So, Mrs. Huber, what
exactly do you want from me?"

"I suspect embezzlement within the company. How
do I go about looking into their files?"

"The little you have to go on does not justify a formal
audit. Your only chance would be if the fellow in Nevada
has sufficient evidence to file a complaint."

Disappointed, I said, "I haven't even located him yet!"

Then he said, "You could call the head of the firm and
seek a voluntary investigation into the company files."

"Good idea. I'll try that for now." And I added, "I'm
sure glad I have a friendly officer I can call for advice!"

"Anytime, Mrs. Huber!"

I picked up the phone again and dialed the number of Lamont & Associates. My status with Monique must have advanced a few notches; I was put through to Mr. Teleford without any fuss.

He said, "Hello, Mrs. Huber. How is your investigation coming along?"

"I'm making some progress. I just came back from paying James Bradley a visit in Ajijic," I answered.

Laughing, he exclaimed, "You don't leave any stones unturned, do you?"

"Actually, my husband and I vacationed in Central Mexico, and we looked Mr. Bradley up in passing."

"How nice for you!"

"Mr. Bradley remembered the name Robert Perdue."

"He actually knows who the man is?"

"He never met him, but he saw the name on paper and identified it as a client's name of Lamont & Associates."

Teleford said, "That's strange. When you called me and asked about a Robert Perdue, I ran the name through my computer and came up empty. How is it spelled?"

"I can't be sure, but I presume P-e-r-d-u-e," I replied.

"That's how I fed it to the computer."

I continued, "Perdue might not be a client of Lamont & Associates at the present time, but may have been four years ago."

"Yes, that's possible, of course."

Then I said, "I suspect embezzlement of some kind. Can the accounting records dating back four or five years be checked?"

I could hear the astonishment in his voice as he said, "I can't believe James Bradley is a crook!" And he added, "Since he admitted to having seen the Perdue guy's name while working for us, how can you suspect him?"

"That might have been a clever move on his part. The way I worded my questions to Mr. Bradley, he had to assume that I already knew Perdue was a client."

"I see." And after a pause, he said, "I still don't believe what you're suggesting, but I'll look into the records. It might take some time to dig them up; we changed our accounting system four years ago."

I said, "Don't you have to save the records for tax purposes?"

"Of course. We have the data; it might just take a while to access." And he added, "As I said, I'll look into it."

"I'd appreciate that very much. Thank you, Mr. Teleford."

After replacing the receiver, I thought, that was nice of him. He could have suggested I go fly a kite! And remembering Walt's kite collection, I smiled to myself.

Chapter 38

I still had the Lamont file in front of me and leafed through it once more. Yes, the file was just the way I had left it before going on the trip. It contained the note to Shelby and the NTSB report; the names, addresses and phone numbers I had gathered; my interview comments list; and the little piece of paper with *Robert Perdue?* written on it.

I re-read all the comments I had made on the list and tried to recall the exact conversation with each person. Then I came to a decision. I picked up the phone once more and dialed.

"Truckee Tahoe Airport. How can I direct your call?"

"Bill Mc Naught, please."

"Who is calling?"

"R.A. Huber." And I added, "He knows me."

"One moment."

There was a lot of clicking in the line. Then, after what seemed like an eternity, I heard a man's voice, "Truckee Police Department, Sergeant Wimbling speaking."

"Officer, I called the airport," I said.

"I know. We intercepted the call. We tried to get in touch with you, R.A. Huber."

"Oh?"

"Why are you calling Bill Mc Naught?"

I started to get annoyed with the officer and said, "I interviewed Mr. Mc Naught two and a half weeks ago, and I'd like to ask him another question. If he's unavailable at the moment, please have him call me back."

Before I could give my number, the sergeant said, "He can't call you back. He's dead."

"Oh! I'm very sorry to hear that. Although old, he looked healthy when I saw him."

"He was murdered."

After I had recovered from the shock, I said, "Are you sure it was murder?"

"He was strangled, Ms Huber!"

"When?"

"Two days ago. On Wednesday afternoon, to be exact."

Then the officer inquired, "What was your interview with Mc Naught about?"

"It was in regards to something that happened four years ago," I said.

"Oh really?" The tone in his voice suggested he didn't believe I was telling the truth.

Then I said, "You mentioned you tried to get in touch with me. Why is that?"

"We found your business card in Mc Naught's overall pocket."

"I see." Then I stated, "I was out of town and just came back last night."

"Are you staying put now?"

"Yes."

"We'll send someone down to your office in the next few days. Make yourself available."

"Yes, sir." And I added, "Can you give me an approximate day? I'm not always at the office."

The sergeant said, "Monday would be the earliest, but it might be at a later date. Do you have a cell phone we can reach you at?"

"Sure," I replied, and gave him the number.

After hanging up, I stared into space for a long time. Poor leprechaun! I stirred things up, and you got murdered as a consequence. I'm so sorry.

I went out the door, leaving it ajar. My office was at ground level of a two-story building. It faced the parking lot, separated by a hedge. There was a space of about three yards between my office door and the hedge. I was seeking that space now, having long ago made it my designated smoking area.

My nerves somewhat restored, I closed the door with chain and padlock and affixed a note, "Back in 10 minutes," in case the repair people showed during my absence. I walked to the Italian Deli around the corner and purchased an antipasto salad to go.

When I returned, before I could take a bite, the phone rang. Picking up the receiver, I was pleased to hear Burt's voice.

"Hi. I got the info for you."

"Wonderful!" I exclaimed.

"Robert Perdue lives in Reno," and he read off the address and phone number. He continued, "There is a roofing business, Perdue and Son, also located in Reno, which probably refers to the same person." He gave me the business address and number as well.

I asked, "Was he the only Robert Perdue you found in Nevada?"

"Yes. I found three Perdues in Las Vegas, and one Claudia Perdue in Reno, but no other Robert."

"You're an absolute jewel, Burt! Thank you so much. I hope I can return the favor soon."

He joked, "Just take me along on your next trip to Mexico!"

Chapter 39

When I had finished my antipasto salad, I called
Robert Perdue's private residence. After a few
rings, an answering machine kicked in. I hung up, not
wanting to leave a message. He was obviously at work, so
I called the number for Perdue and Son.

"Good afternoon, Perdue and Son," said a pleasant,
young-sounding female voice.

"Mr. Robert Perdue, please."

"Who's calling?"

"R.A. Huber." And I added, "He doesn't know me."

"Oh, you'd like him to come to your house and give
an estimate. I schedule all his appointments. Let me see
- - We can make it next Wednesday or Thursday, or if you
prefer - -"

I interrupted her flow and asked, "Could I talk to Mr.
Perdue personally? I have a few questions."

"Sure. I think he just walked in. One moment,
please."

When I got the man on the line, I said, "You are Robert
Perdue, correct?"

"Yes, ma'am. And you are?"

"R.A. Huber, Private Detective," I replied.

Chuckling, he said, "I guess detectives need new roofs
too!"

"I'm not calling about a roof, Mr. Perdue. I'm
investigating an event that happened four years ago, and
I'd like to make an appointment to discuss the matter."

"Oh, my girl at the front desk said you were a
prospective new customer."

I liked this man! He obviously could not be bothered with trifles like political correctness, and called his receptionist 'girl.'

"I might have misled her; sorry about that." And I continued, "You were a client of the brokerage firm Lamont and Associates four years ago. Is that right?"

"Yes, they were my brokers," he replied.

"And you are aware that Steven Lamont perished in a plane crash flying out of Truckee?"

"Of course. It was in all the papers at the time."

Then I stated, "I understand you talked to Mr. Lamont the day before his crash."

"I wonder how you figured that out, but yes, I did. We ran into each other after skiing, and met for a drink later on." Then he said, "Now please get to the point and tell me what your investigation is all about and what it has to do with me."

"I have reason to believe the plane crash was not accidental."

Clearly astonished, he said, "What are you talking about? You're not suggesting foul play?"

"I'm afraid that is *exactly* what I'm suggesting, Mr. Perdue."

After a pause, he said, "It was hard enough to digest when I heard of Steven and Claire's fatal accident, but now that you propose it was murder, I feel even worse."

I inquired, "I noticed you called them by their first names. Did you actually know both Mr. and Mrs. Lamont?"

"Yes. We were good friends."

I was surprised at this revelation but refrained from commenting.

Then I continued, "As I said, I'd like to make an appointment to talk to you in person, as soon as possible, if I may."

"Sure, I'll talk to you. I doubt I can be of any help with your investigation, but you can give me a try." Then he asked, "Are you a local?"

"No," I said, "I'm from the L.A. area."

"When are you planning to come?"

"As soon as you can give me an appointment," I replied.

"Hold on, I'll get the schedule from the front desk," and he put me on hold.

He was back in a flash and said, "Okay, here we are." He murmured several appointment times to himself, and then said more audibly, "I'm scheduled to make a few estimates at several locations early Monday morning, but I should be back at my office by eleven at the latest. Or I could see you at two in the afternoon. So if you're ready to fly up on Monday, it's your pick: 11:00 a.m. or 2:00 p.m."

I considered, and then said, "If it's all the same to you, I'd prefer the afternoon."

He gave me directions from the Reno airport to his place of business, and we ended the call.

Chapter 40

By mid-afternoon the door repairs were in full swing. I sat at my desk, trying to ignore the banging and drilling noises. Once again I stared at the file in front of me. As far as I could see, it contained no significant illuminating facts. And how could the perpetrator even be sure I kept a file on the case? The break-in made no sense! Unless, - - *yes, of course!* - - I nodded to myself.

Again, I pondered every conversation with each person. Then I weighed my theory against everything I had learned, and yes, I deduced, it all fit in.

I had to act fast, before anyone else got killed.

The noise from the drill was at a crescendo, so I resorted to making my next call by cell phone in the parking lot.

I rang Perdue back and said, "Mr. Perdue, could I possibly see you on the weekend rather than on Monday?"

"Oh?"

"I have a reason for the change, which I'll explain when I see you in person."

"Your talk with me is that urgent?"

"Absolutely."

After a pause, he agreed, "All right. I can't see you tomorrow, but I could manage Sunday."

"That would be great. Thank you!"

Just before we hung up, I cautioned, "And please, Mr. Perdue, be alert in the next couple of days; I have reason to believe you might be in danger."

"You've got to be kidding!"

"I am serious. A man I talked to regarding this case was murdered two days ago."

Chapter 41

In the evening I discussed the events of the day with Peter.

When I got to the part about Bill Mc Naught, he said, "Are you blaming yourself for his death?"

I nodded.

After a lengthy silence, he said, "What were you going to ask Mc Naught?"

"Never mind. I'm obviously too late to ask him anything," and I continued to divulge the rest of my phone conversations.

Then Peter remarked, "So you located Perdue in Reno?"

"Yes, thanks to good old Burt." And I added, "I warned Perdue that he might be in danger. I hope he takes my warning seriously."

"Really?"

"What do you mean by 'really'?" I asked.

"Do you truly believe Perdue is in any danger?"

"Yes, I do." Then I said, "Do you feel like doing an overnighter with me in Reno this Sunday?"

"I can't, Regula. This is the weekend of my book-signing event."

"Oh, of course. I totally forgot!"

Smiling, he observed, "There are other things in my life besides your case!" And getting serious, he asked, "Have you looked into flight schedules yet?"

"I've decided to drive."

Raising an eyebrow, he said, "Is that practical for an overnighter? It's a nine-hour drive; you'll spend most of your time on the road!"

"It's extremely impractical, I know."

"So?"

"I can't very well pack my pistol in the carry-on, so I'll have to drive."

"I see!"

After a pause, Peter said, "I hate to have you do the long, boring drive by yourself."

"I'll be fine."

"When are you leaving?"

"In the middle of the night." And I added, "I have tomorrow to run errands and do household chores. I would've liked to work out at the gym, but I can't fit it in at this point."

He said, "We got plenty of exercise hiking up hills all over Central Mexico."

"That's not the same."

He chafed, "I know. You need more of a physical challenge to stimulate *body and mind!*" Then he became grave and asked, "You're getting close to solving your case, aren't you?"

I nodded.

"You've narrowed it down to one suspect. Am I right?"

"Yes."

He looked at me questioningly and said, "Are you going to let me in on your findings?"

I replied, "I'd rather not share my theory until I get a better picture. I might be wrong."

"You'll get 'the picture' in Reno?"

"One way or another, yes."

My hubby eyed me intently, saying with obvious anxiety, "Please be extremely careful, Regula!"

Chapter 42

The alarm went off at 2:00 a.m. Sunday morning. I knew if I lingered in bed just a few seconds, I'd fall back to sleep. So groggy and disoriented, I stumbled into the bathroom. Moments later, I blindly felt my way down the hall toward the kitchen. A glass of orange juice, followed by a piece of toast and a cup of coffee, revived my senses somewhat. Then a prolonged shower restored me to some degree of alertness.

An hour later I bent over Peter, still in dreamland, and whispered in his ear, "I'm leaving now."

He made some snorting noises but did not respond. I kissed him on the forehead and tiptoed out of the room.

As expected, the drive to Reno was uneventful and boring. My mind flashed back to the previous day. While Peter spent his first day of the weekend's book-signing event at the local Barnes & Noble store, I was doing household chores and running errands. In the late afternoon I made an attempt to check base with the Lamont siblings. I left a message on Michelle's answering machine, telling her I had located Robert Perdue in Reno and would call her upon my return. I smiled to myself recalling the conversation I had after dialing the Prescott number. Scott's Aunt Suzanne answered. There was an awful lot of background noise.

I said, "Mrs. Prescott? This is R.A. Huber. Can I talk to Scott please?"

She shouted, "Speak up! I can't hear you!"

I raised my voice, "Is Scott handy?"

"No. He's in the middle of a soccer game."

That explained all the noise. I said, "I called your residence."

"Of course you did! I'm on call for work on Saturdays, so I'm obligated to have it switched to the darned cell phone."

I was just going to reply when she shouted, "Attaboy, Scott! - - Yea! - - Don't lose the ball - - good footwork - - there's a loophole - - Yes! - - Go - - go - - goal!" I could visualize the lively redhead cheering and bouncing up and down. Tremendous applause and clapping sounds nearly punctured my eardrums through the line.

I said, "Did Scott just make a goal?"

"He sure did!"

"What's the score?"

"One to one."

"Congratulations!" I said.

She yelled, "The game isn't over yet!"

"Tell Scott congratulations, anyhow! Tell him I'll call again soon."

"What?"

"Never mind, Mrs. Prescott." And I quickly added, "I'm rooting for Scott's team," and hung up.

Then I reflected earnestly about Scott and Michelle and hoped that soon I could help bring closure to the tragic death of their parents.

A few minutes past noon I pulled into the Harrah's Hotel parking structure in downtown Reno. My appointment with Mr. Perdue was not until three, so I had some leisure time. I had lunch first and then checked into my room. I'm not one for taking naps, but just resting on the bed felt refreshing. I had mulled over the Lamont case for nine hours on my drive up, so by that point I needed to empty my brain and just relax.

Chapter 43

Robert Perdue had suggested meeting at his office, since it would be easier for me to find than his residence. Once I was on the correct street, I didn't even have to search for the number; I spotted the big sign, *Perdue & Son*, half a block away. We both pulled into the parking lot at the same time.

We introduced ourselves, and while shaking hands, he grinned and exclaimed, "*You're* a private eye?"

"I'm tougher than I look." Then I said, "Thank you for seeing me on a Sunday."

A pair of mischievous blue eyes looked down at me. His face was round and friendly topped by blondish hair thinning at the crown. He was a muscular man about six feet two inches tall and in his forties. He was dressed casually in a pair of jeans and a light-blue polo shirt.

I followed him to the two-story building. He unlocked the door, flicked on some light switches, and then motioned me to enter. We were in a small lobby with a hallway straight ahead and an elevator to our right.

He pushed the elevator button and commented, "On the ground level we have the stock-rooms and garages housing the trucks. The offices are on the second floor."

As we stepped from the elevator on the second story, we found ourselves in a small foyer consisting of a reception desk winged by a waiting area. We walked passed the reception area and down a hallway. Perdue opened a door to our left, strode to the window and adjusted the vertical blinds to let the sunlight in. At the far corner of the room a small table and chair were set up facing shelves loaded with roof sample-books. We walked to the opposite side of the room where he directed me into a chair in front of a large oak desk and then seated himself behind it.

I asked, "Are you the *son*?"

He stared and then said, "Oh, I see. Of Perdue & Son, you mean?"

I nodded.

"Yes, Father started the business. He retired a few years ago."

"How many people do you employ?"

He replied, "Let's see. I have a man who helps me with giving estimates and customer consultations. The rest of the office staff consists of the receptionist, a woman that takes care of billing and secretarial work, and a part-time accountant. Most of my employees are roofers. They're the ones that do the manual work of installing the roofs and also repair existing roofs. We currently have four teams of five men each. So that's a total of twenty workers."

With an engaging smile, he added, "If push comes to shove, I can jump in and help with the manual labor."

I liked this uncomplicated man. I had already been partial to him during our phone conversations, but the more I got to know him, the more I was impressed.

I came to the point and said, "As you already know, I'm investigating the plane crash of Mr. and Mrs. Lamont. I have good reason to believe the crash was not accidental."

He said, "I've been thinking about this ever since you called. Why didn't the authorities conduct a homicide investigation at the time?"

"It's a long story, but something came to light recently that makes murder probable. I've had to backtrack step by step, and finally ended up at your door, so to speak." And I continued, "We've already established that you were a client of Lamont & Associates four years ago. I understand you met with Steven Lamont the day before his fatal crash."

He nodded, stating, "Yes, that's right."

"You also told me that you were friends with the Lamonts. Your talk that day with Steven Lamont, was it business related or of a private matter?"

He said, "I'd better explain my relationship with Steve. I'd known Steve for a long time. He and I went to school together."

"High school?"

"No, college."

"Oh."

He smiled and said, "You probably think a college education is wasted on a roofer, but actually my business degree comes in handy at times. My father, a very intelligent man, never finished high school. He wanted me to have a good education even though we both knew I'd end up in the family business.

"As I said, I met Steve at college and we became good friends. He was already dating Claire at the time, so I knew her as well. We kept in contact over the years but didn't see each other frequently; we lived too far apart. When Steve started his brokerage firm, I had a little money to invest and used him as my stockbroker. Later, when his firm grew, I still used Lamont & Associates as my brokers."

"I see." Then I asked, "Was Steven Lamont still handling your account four years ago?"

"No," he said, "my account had been delegated to other brokers at Lamont & Associates long before that time."

"Please continue."

"You wanted to know what I talked to Steve about that evening. A week prior, I received a statement from Lamont and Associates that had me totally puzzled. It just didn't make sense to me. I felt there had to be a mistake with the figures. It looked like I'd lost a sizeable amount of money in a totally unfamiliar investment. I felt sure there must have been an error in the statement. I was going to call the firm and have the statement explained to me. So when I ran into my friend after skiing, I figured I might as well ask him about it, and we decided to meet for a drink later."

"And what did Mr. Lamont say?"

"He was furious! Then he wanted exact details of the statement, and I tried to remember them as best I could."

"Furious?" I asked.

"He was absolutely livid and had a hard time controlling his emotions. I had never seen Steve so mad."

"Did he say who he was mad at?"

"No."

I said, "Mr. Perdue, please try to remember the exact words spoken by you and Mr. Lamont after you had told him what was in the statement."

He reflected and then said, "It's so long ago, and I can't possibly remember the exact words. He asked me who handled my account. Frankly, I didn't know because it wasn't always the same person. I tried to calm him down and told him it could just be a bookkeeping error and be easily straightened out. Steve was adamant. He was not convinced that it had been just an innocent mistake. I remember him mumbling to himself something like ...'not the first time,' and 'son of a bitch.' Then he seemed to get control of himself. He said he'd look into the problem and get back to me the following week."

After a long pause, I said, "Did you know that Mr. Lamont cut his ski vacation short and attempted to fly back to Los Angeles to investigate the matter?"

"I wasn't aware of that." Then he exclaimed, "Oh God! Do you think he was killed because of what we discussed?"

"It's entirely possible," I said.

Mr. Perdue looked at me incredulously and then said, "But that doesn't make sense! I got a letter attached to a new statement from Lamont & Associates soon afterwards, informing me the first statement had been sent in error."

"How interesting! Do you still do business with Lamont & Associates?"

"No, I use a different brokerage firm now. Somehow, after Steve's death, I didn't feel I owed them any loyalty and found a firm here in town."

"Did you keep their records?"

"Sure. The file ought to be around." He got up and said, "Come, let's see."

I followed him into an office across the hall. He scrutinized the file cabinets standing against the wall. Pointing at the long row of drawers, he said, "These are current files; no use in looking here." He glanced around and spotted a lone file cabinet with only three drawers. They were marked "Closed Files, A – I, J – R and S - Z."

He rummaged through the middle drawer and then said, "Here we are," pulling out the Lamont & Associates folder.

Opening it, he asked, "What exactly are we looking for?"

"I'd like to see the statement in question and also the corrected one with the letter attached," I said.

He found the documents and handed them to me. I read the first statement carefully, but since I was not a financial genius and had no clue as to stock statements, it meant nothing to me. I looked at the corrected statement and noticed that the figure $250,000 noted on the first document was no longer present. Other than that, this statement did not mean anything to me either. What I was most interested in was the attached letter. Actually, it was not a proper letter. Although it had been typed on Lamont & Associates stationary, it was short and unsigned. In other words, it was just a note, and it read:

"Please disregard our previous statement. There has been a client mix-up in the former statement, and we apologize. The revised and current statement attached is the correct document."

I looked up at Perdue and mused, "Our killer is cunning!"

He said, "What do you mean?"

"He sent a corrected statement, preventing you from making a fuss. He cleverly attached a note with a plausible explanation, being careful not to sign the note!"

"How can you be sure what the note states is not the truth? I really took it as a fact that the whole thing had been a simple mistake."

I nodded, saying, "That's the whole point! It was artfully done; a simple little note to satisfy you that it had all been a mistake, and now stood corrected!"

Then I said, "I would advise you to make copies of these documents and take one set home with you. They will be needed by the police as evidence to justify an audit at Lamont & Associates."

"You're very sure of yourself, Mrs. Huber!" he stated.

"Yes, at this point I think I am," I replied.

"Okay, I'll make copies," he agreed. And he added, "Are you suggesting someone might break in here and steal the file?"

"It's a possibility. My office has been broken into recently."

There was a copy machine in the room, and he proceeded to make copies of the documents. Then he placed the originals back in the file, folded the copies and tucked them away in his jeans' back pocket.

We made our way back to his office, and then he said, "When you called you were also telling me that I might be in danger. Are you serious?"

"Absolutely. That's why we have to take measures, you and I."

"I have no idea what you're talking about," he said, "but let's have some refreshments first; I'm dying of thirst. I can offer you Coke, beer, coffee or water."

"Water would be great, thank you."

He walked over to a small refrigerator by the door and then handed me a bottle of water and opened a can of beer for himself.

Chapter 44

Thus settled, we got down to business.

Perdue said, "Let's assume there was something fishy going on with my statements at the time. But my dear lady, since I never got wise to it four years ago, what makes you think the person responsible would assume I'd take action now? I mean, how could I possibly be in any danger four years after the fact?"

I replied, "The murderer might find it crucial to silence you before he thinks you'd have a chance to talk to me."

He thought about this for a moment and then said, "Oh, now I know why you were in such a hurry to come and see me!"

I said, "The way I look at it, the most probable time for an attack on you would be this weekend and the next few days." And I added, "Actually, tomorrow would be the most likely day."

He said, "Do you know who it is?"

"Yes, I'm pretty sure I know."

"Why don't you go to the police?"

"I don't have enough proof. And there is a slight possibility that I'm wrong."

Then I said, "Have you kept your eyes open since my phone call on Friday?"

"Huh?"

"Did anyone follow you around, for example?"

"Oh, I see what you mean. No, I didn't notice anything or anyone suspicious," he said.

After a pause, I asked, "What kind of estimate appointments do you have scheduled in the next few days?"

Perplexed, he said, "You don't think someone - -"

I interrupted, "Yes, precisely! The killer could pose as a prospective customer."

He stared, and then he got to his feet, saying, "I'll get the appointment schedule. Be right back."

When he returned we scrutinized the entries. On Monday, April 19, there were entries at 7:00 a.m., at 8:30 a.m. and at 9:45 a.m. A customer name, location address and phone number followed each of these times entered. Then at 11:00 a.m., there was just a name, "Raymond Wilson - - our office." At 2:00 p.m. the appointment for "R.A. Huber - - our office," was crossed out. There were two more entries with location addresses for Monday afternoon, the first at 3:30 p.m. and the last at 5:00 p.m.

I looked over the rest of the week's schedules, and then I asked, "Are all these appointments yours, or do you share them with the other person that gives estimates?"

"They're all mine. The other guy has his own appointment schedule," he replied.

I said, "I notice that, except for Raymond Wilson at 11:00 a.m. Monday and mine at 2:00 p.m. which is crossed out, all the appointments for the entire week have location addresses. So am I right in presuming it's unusual for a prospective customer to come to your office for a consultation?"

Perdue stated, "It's not unusual. There are people who prefer to look at samples before they get an estimate."

"How does it work with the majority of customers? What I mean is, explain the process to me, please."

"Prospective customers usually call for estimates. Most of them have an idea of what they're interested in, in terms of type, quality, and color of a roof. The receptionist normally schedules an appointment, and either the other fellow or I will drive to the respective residential or business address. We need to see the house or building in order to make an estimate. I usually take two or three different types of sample-books along, so I have something to show the customer."

I pointed at the shelves behind the little table and asked, "Are those the books?"

"Yes," he said, "they're miniature samples of roofing material."

"Sorry I interrupted. Please continue."

He went on, "Most people get several estimates from different roofing companies to compare prices and quality of material. Then, if the customer chooses us, we'll get another call, and a date and time is appointed for the actual installation of the roof."

I asked, "So most customers do not come into your office and look at the sample-books?"

"Actually, quite a few do. Most of them do so because they have a hard time deciding what color and texture to select for a roof on their home."

"But they would generally come here after you had gone to their house?" I asked.

"Most frequently, yes. But it's not unusual for a prospective customer to want to look at what we have to offer first."

Then I asked, "Who decides which estimates are given by whom?"

"Pardon?"

I laughed and said, "I'm expressing myself poorly. I meant is it left up to the receptionist to assign you or your assistant for giving the estimate?"

"I get you! Yes, the receptionist looks at both our calendars and makes the decision, unless someone specifically asks for one or the other of us."

"Does that happen often?" I inquired.

"Does what happen often?"

"That someone would ask specifically for either you or your assistant?"

"Not often, but it happens." And he added, "In my case it is usually older folks who've heard of the roofing company way back when my dad was in charge, and they still like the idea of doing business with the owner."

I looked at Monday's entries in front of us again, saying, "During our first phone conversation you gave me the option of either an 11:00 a.m. or 2:00 p.m. appointment for tomorrow, and I chose the afternoon time."

I could tell he had no idea where I was going with this. He probably thought, what difference does that make now? But he said politely, "Yes?"

"So this Raymond Wilson must have made the 11:00 a.m. appointment after our phone conversation."

Perdue grinned and said, "I'm starting to see you're a darned good lady detective!"

"Did you talk to him yourself?"

"No."

"Did he ask for you specifically?"

"I don't know. This Raymond Wilson is news to me too. I haven't looked at my schedule since I talked to you on Friday. Shortly after your second call, I took off for my last estimate that day, and then went straight home."

"Could you ask your receptionist for specifics about Mr. Wilson first thing tomorrow morning for me," I inquired.

He said, "I can do better than that," and reached for the phone.

He dialed a number and then said, "Hi, honey. It's me. Is Tammie around?"

He listened, and then commented, "Oh yes, I forgot. I'll try her cell phone. See you soon."

He entered another number, and then I heard him say, "Hi, Tam." And then, "Of course I'm not spying on you! This is business. Listen. Think back to Friday afternoon. Do you remember a guy by the name of Raymond Wilson making an appointment to see me in my office tomorrow?"

He nodded into the receiver and then ordered, "Tell me the exact conversation you had with him."

He listened carefully and then asked, "That's it?" And after a short pause he said, "Thanks Tam! You can go back to your date now!"

He put the receiver back on the hook and grimaced, saying, "Teenagers always think you're checking up on them!"

"Your daughter?" I asked.

"Yes."

Then I chuckled and said, "So when you referred to *your girl* at the front desk, you literally meant your girl!"

With a puzzled look on his face he said, "Of course." Then he laughed, and stated, "I'm a pretty laid-back guy, but even I would hesitate to call my office help 'girl'!" And he continued, "Our receptionist was on vacation last week. My daughter, Tammie, helped us out by taking the receptionist's place during high school spring break."

I said, "So what did Tammie remember about Raymond Wilson?"

"That he wanted to talk to me. Then Tammie asked him if it concerned an estimate. Wilson answered with a 'yes,' but needed to talk to me first. Tammie then told him I was out and asked for his phone number so I could call him back. He stated that wasn't necessary, but could he make an appointment to see me Monday morning as early as possible. Tammie looked at the schedules and informed him that the earliest time with me would be 11:00 a.m., but my assistant could see him at 9:00 a.m. Mr. Wilson said he wanted to do business with Mr. Perdue personally, and that 11:00 a.m. would be fine."

We looked at each other in silence for some time, and then I stated, "I think the man calling himself Raymond Wilson is our villain." And I added, "Give me a moment to reflect on a plan of action."

I finally asked, "Do you own a gun, Mr. Perdue?"

"A gun? Are you kidding? I've always thought I could take care of myself without one."

"Never mind; I carry one."

He raised his eyebrows and asked, "Where?"

"At the moment the pistol is in my purse, but tomorrow it'll be handy."

After a long pause, I said, "All right, here is what we'll do," and I laid the entire plan before him.

He heard me out and then said, "Is all that really necessary? I mean I'm a good-sized man. I'm sure I can take care of myself on a one-to-one basis."

"Remember, we're dealing with a killer here. He murdered Mr. and Mrs. Lamont four years ago, and in all probability recently killed another human being. If I'm correct in my deductions, you're next on his agenda and he's planning to do the deed tomorrow."

Then he said, "What if Raymond Wilson is just a harmless guy in the market for a new roof? Wouldn't we both look like fools?"

"I'll only come out into the open if you were to be jeopardized."

"Okay," he agreed, still reluctant.

I asked, "Do we have a deal?"

"Yes, Mrs. Huber, we do."

We shook hands on it, and I left his office.

Chapter 45

Monday I arrived at Perdue & Son at 10:30 in the morning. I found a middle-aged receptionist on the second floor.

She asked, "Mrs. Huber?"

"Yes, I am she," I said.

"Mr. Perdue is not back from his morning appointment yet. He said I should make you comfortable. Would you like some coffee?" And pointing to the waiting area, she added, "Have a seat."

If this Raymond Wilson should be early for his appointment, I certainly needed to avoid running into him in the reception area.

So I said, "No coffee, thank you. Can I wait in Mr. Perdue's office, please?"

"Surely, if you prefer."

"Thanks! I know the way."

I established myself in Perdue's office. I first stashed my purse out of sight on the floor behind his desk. Then I kept myself entertained by leafing through a couple of the sample-books. Perdue found me with a heavy volume in hand at 10.45 a.m.

He winked at me, asking, "Not in position yet, R.A. Huber?"

"You're not taking this seriously, are you?"

"Actually, I am. Joking helps me get over the tension."

I looked at my watch and said, "He might be early."

"Don't worry, I told the receptionist not to bring him in until exactly 11:00 a.m. We should probably not talk anymore, though. He wasn't out front when I passed the area, but he might get there at any moment."

I nodded my head and then we waited in silence. At two minutes before eleven we took our positions. The front of the big desk was made of solid wood. I went behind it, took my loaded .25 pistol out of the purse, and crawled into the desk's leg-room. Perdue seated himself in his desk chair. I felt a little crunched beside his long legs, but I wasn't too uncomfortable, at least not for the time being.

We didn't have to wait long. At precisely eleven, I heard the receptionist's voice in the hallway, "This way, please." Then I heard the door open and someone's entering footsteps, and the door closing again. Perdue's knee hit my elbow as he got to his feet.

I heard them introducing themselves, and I assumed they shook hands. Then Perdue's legs appeared next to me again as he sat back down.

Perdue asked, "You're interested in installing a new roof?"

The man calling himself Raymond Wilson said, "Yes. Thanks for seeing me so promptly. I'm sure you're busy this time of year with the rainy season coming to an end."

"I can't complain, but actually, our busiest season is in the fall when people suddenly remember that they had some leaks the previous winter!"

As I started to feel a little cramped in my "cubbyhole," I wished they would hurry up and get to the point soon.

Then Perdue said, "Are you looking into installing a new roof at a residence or a business?"

"Oh, it's for our home. The house has a square footage of 2,400 feet," the man replied.

"I'll still have to see the house before I can give you a proper estimate."

The Wilson fellow said, "I understand that, of course. I just wanted to get an idea first of the materials and colors you have readily available. My wife is rather picky and I kind of have an idea what she wants."

To my relief Perdue finally got up, saying, "Let's look through some samples."

I heard them walk over to the "sample corner" at the other side of the room. Careful not to make a sound, I peeked around one side of the desk. Both men had their backs turned to me. They were about the same height. All I could detect about the man calling himself Wilson was a mop of white hair, since he faced the other direction. He wore a navy blazer and gray trousers. They hovered over the sample-books at the little table, with Perdue explaining quality and texture of each miniature roofing material. Both were standing, neither one making use of the chair in front of the table. I noticed that as Perdue was turning the pages, the other man was careful not to touch anything.

Having gone through three different books, the visitor shook his head and then said, "We haven't come across the type of roofing material my spouse has in mind. It's thicker and has more of a raised texture to it than what you've shown me so far." And he added, "My wife is an invalid, and I'd like to please her."

Perdue said, "Sorry to hear that." And he continued, "I think I know now what she is aiming for," and he reached for a book on the top shelf.

At the precise moment Perdue had his arms extended getting at the book, the other man stepped behind him and quickly extracted a piece of electrical cord from his blazer pocket. In a swift motion he swung the cord over Perdue's head, holding on to the ends with each hand. In a split second the cord was around Perdue's throat and neck, and the man pulled it tight. Perdue, taken by surprise, let go of the sample-book which landed on the floor with a thud.

I stepped out from behind the desk and with my pistol pointed at the man, I shouted, "Oh no, you don't, Mr. Teleford!"

He let go of the cord and swung around. He stared at me, then at the pistol aimed at him.

I said, "The gray wig and the glasses might disguise you somewhat, but I recognized your voice the minute you opened your mouth!"

Teleford's expression changed from surprise to cold fury as he shouted, "I drove all night to beat you to it, you bitch --" He was going to say more, but caught himself and fell silent.

Without moving, and keeping my aim at Teleford, I nodded to Perdue, "Are you okay?"

Rubbing his throat, he said, "I'm shaken up a little, but I'm fine."

Then I motioned to Teleford. "Turn the customer chair around to face me and have a seat."

He didn't move and said, "Why should I?"

I repeated, "Turn the chair around and sit down."

He eyed the weapon pointed at him and did as he was told.

Then I said to Perdue, "Will you do us the honor, please?"

"With pleasure," he said, and stepping behind his desk, he took out a huge roll of duct-tape from the top drawer. Then he proceeded to tape Teleford firmly into the chair, making sure his arms and legs were taped down so he could not move or get up.

Teleford tried to fight him off and protested, "What the hell do you think you're doing?"

Perdue said, "We are making a citizen's arrest and want to make sure you don't bolt out of here."

I stepped closer, and my pistol pointed at his forehead, I said, "You had better hold nice and still so Mr. Perdue can do a good job."

Teleford glared at me, saying, "You wouldn't have the guts to pull the trigger, Huber!"

I looked him straight in the eye. "Don't provoke me, or you'll soon find out."

Our eyes locked for a few seconds, and Teleford was the first to avert his. By the time Perdue was done with the job, Teleford looked like a mummy. The mouth was not taped; we wanted him to be able to talk.

I finally lowered my pistol, and Perdue called the Reno Police Department.

Teleford said, "This is outrageous!"

"Murder is what's outrageous," I stated.

He said, "What are you talking about? How are you going to justify your capturing and tying me down to the police? I'll tell them you threatened me and I acted in self defense."

"Good try, Mr. Teleford, but not good enough by a long shot. First you put on a silly wig and glasses in an attempt at a disguise. Then you just happened to have a piece of electrical cord in your pocket in case someone might attack you and you needed to defend yourself! No, that won't do; you'll have to come up with a better story."

And I continued, "It is a fact that you were in the process of strangling Mr. Perdue, when I stopped you just in time." And pointing at Perdue's neck, I went on, "And he has the cord marks to proof it!"

"That's attempted murder at the very most," Teleford snapped back.

I stated, "You and I both know that you murdered three human beings already, and that Mr. Perdue here would have been your fourth victim."

"You can't prove that! You haven't got a shred of evidence," he said, glaring at me.

I tried a bluff, "You were seen at the crime scene in Truckee."

"You're lying," he shouted, "I was wearing –" he caught himself and continued, "I am sure no one saw me anywhere near his house!"

I raised an eyebrow and said, "Do you mean near Bill Mc Naught's house?"

He realized what a blunder he had just made and kept silent.

Then I said, "Thanks for informing me of the fact that Bill Mc Naught was murdered at his house. Until now, all I knew was that he had been strangled, but I didn't know where!"

"Didn't you just imply that someone had seen me at the murder scene in Truckee?"

"I was referring to the murder of Steven and Claire Lamont." I commented.

He sneered at me and said, "And what would you know about that?"

I had him totally riled by now, so I went for another shot in the dark.

I looked at him knowingly and stated, "It's simple to contaminate the fuel in the tanks of a small airplane, like the Cessna 152!"

That's when he totally went berserk. He yelled, "You nasty old bitch! I should have taken care of you right away, but I didn't think - -"

I interrupted, "Yes, Mr. Teleford, you didn't think I posed a real threat to you. Never underestimate this little old lady from Pasadena!"

At that point we heard sirens, and the authorities were soon to take over.

Chapter 46

A t 1:30 that afternoon, I was having lunch with Robert Perdue in a restaurant in walking distance of his business. We ate in agreeable silence for a while, and I pondered on the last two and a half hours. After Thomas Teleford had been escorted out of the office handcuffed, the remaining Reno police officials took Perdue's statement and gathered evidence. It mainly consisted of the electrical cord, which Teleford had dropped on the floor, copies of the Lamont & Associates documents from four years ago, and several photos one of the officers had taken of Perdue's neck from different angles.

When the officers were about to take my statement, I told them that mine was a long story. I also mentioned that it might not be a bad idea to have Sergeant Wimbling of the Truckee Police Department there as a witness to my statement, or at least provide him with a copy of it. They were skeptical at first, but I insisted that today's case was tied to the murder of Truckee resident Bill Mc Naught, killed last Wednesday. I pointed out that it would save the Truckee police a trip to Los Angeles, and by the same token I would not have to tell my story twice. That seemed to make sense to the Reno officials, and they told me to come and give my statement at their headquarters. I begged them to let me have some lunch first since I was starving. So I was to report at the police station at three o'clock sharp.

Perdue eyed me across the table, and commented, "For a slender lady, you sure are doing a good job of downing that big sandwich!"

I laughed and stated, "Confrontations always make me hungry. Thanks for inviting me!"

"You saved my life! The least I can do is buy your lunch," he joked.

Then getting serious, he said, "I was totally taken by surprise. The guy acted so genuinely interested in a new roof. He seemed sincere when he told me about the invalid wife. By the time I reached for that last book, I had come to the conclusion that you were barking up the wrong tree, and this Raymond Wilson was simply a prospective customer."

I said, "Yes, I understand that he sounded convincing to you. On the other hand, I recognized his voice right away and knew what was coming."

Then he stated, "I don't understand Teleford's charade with the disguise. I mean he and I had never met, and he couldn't possibly have known that you would be present. So what was the point of the wig and granny-glasses?"

I said, "He wanted to be described as an older, white-haired man with glasses. Don't forget, when he called for the appointment he knew that a receptionist would see him come and leave your office, and maybe other personnel as well. I'm sure he wanted to frame the former accountant of Lamont & Associates, who is a gray-haired man of 66 and wears glasses." And I continued, "From the little slip he made today when I provoked him, I gathered that he most likely also wore the wig and glasses when he murdered Bill Mc Naught."

Then he looked at me pensively and said, "I believe you would have pulled that trigger if you had to!"

"Absolutely," I said.

After a pause, he went on, "This might sound rude, but I'm really curious. How old are you, Mrs. Huber?"

"I'm 61 years young."

"You probably never want to retire?"

"I already am retired," I said.

"Come again?"

"My husband and I both retired over two years ago. A few months later I started the detective business as sort of a hobby. I've enjoyed being a sleuth ever since."

"And a darned good one, as far as I can judge," he commented.

Then he asked, "Is your husband part of the business too?"

"I sometimes discuss my cases with him, and he occasionally provides me with valuable insight. To answer your question, no, he isn't really part of the business. He has his own hobby."

"What's that?"

"He's a writer, and starting to show some success as such," I said proudly.

"What kind of writer?"

"He mostly writes biographies, but he's also dabbled in fiction. I suspect his current book is near completion."

"What's it about?"

"I have no idea; he keeps it a secret!"

Perdue laughed out loud and exclaimed, "I'd like to meet him!"

Chapter 47

I was in a soul-searching mood while driving to the Reno Police Station. I had answered Perdue's question about being able to pull the trigger without hesitation. But the truth of the matter was, I had never really been put to the test. Before I opened my detective agency I had gone through extensive target shooting training and consequently turned out to be a capable shot, but I had never actually shot a human being. Thank God, threatening to do so had sufficed so far. I presumed that if I found myself in a situation with no other choice, I would pull the trigger, but I hoped I'd be spared the experience.

At the police station I was ushered into a room where two officers whom I had met earlier, and another law enforcer introduced as Sergeant Wimbling from the Truckee police, waited for me. I gave my statement, telling them everything I knew about the case as well as what I suspected. I told the entire story, starting with Scott Lamont coming to my office with the draft letter, and ending with catching Thomas Teleford red-handed attempting to strangle Robert Perdue.

When I had finished, one of the officers said, "How did you come to the conclusion that fuel contamination caused the plane crash?"

I smiled and said, "That was actually a guess, but judging by Teleford's reaction when I suggested it to him this morning, I was right on target."

He nodded. Then he asked, "How did you figure out that Teleford would come to Reno to silence Mr. Perdue?"

I replied, "My office was broken into while I was in Mexico. Nothing was stolen and I felt sure the break-in had to do with my case. The day after my return from Mexico I was in my office making several phone calls. One of my calls was to Mr. Perdue, scheduling an appointment to see him on Monday. It occurred to me that the reason for breaking into my office might have been to bug it."

"Did you find the bug?"

"I didn't bother to look for the device; I wouldn't know what to search for, having never seen one," I said.

All three men appeared to be amused by the fact that I had never seen a bug.

I continued, "It seems I was correct in my hunch. Teleford certainly didn't expect me to arrive at Perdue & Son until two in the afternoon."

Then I was asked, "What was the motive for the crimes, in your opinion?"

"I suspect that Teleford committed some kind of embezzlement or fraud on part of the Lamont & Associates clientele. Then, when Steven Lamont got wise to his actions and planned to look into the records and expose him, he resorted to murder."

The officer said, "We're ordering a thorough investigation and audit of the Lamont & Associates accounts dating back to four years ago and beyond. Something definitely looked deceitful about the documents we collected from Mr. Perdue."

Sergeant Wimbling opened his mouth for the first time and asked, "What were you going to ask Bill Mc Naught when I intercepted your call?"

I said, "When I first interviewed Mr. Mc Naught I questioned him about having seen anything or anyone suspicious around the plane or airport. His answer was that he hadn't seen any strangers or anyone suspicious hanging around. The day you intercepted my call, I had gone over all my notes, and it occurred to me that Mr. Mc Naught might have only considered a stranger as being suspicious. So I was going to ask him if he had seen anyone he knew hanging around."

The sergeant asked, "Thomas Teleford was not a stranger to him?"

"No. They knew each other."

After a pause, I inquired, "Can I ask you something, Sergeant?"

"Sure."

"What was the circumstance of Mr. Mc Naught's murder?"

"I thought I had already told you; he was strangled."

"Yes, you told me that. What I mean is, was he also strangled with an electric cord?"

"Yes."

"Where was he killed?"

The sergeant replied, "In front of the victim's house. Why do you ask?"

I said, "Teleford made a slip today and told me no one could have seen him anywhere near Mc Naught's house. Since up to that moment I had assumed that Mr. Mc Naught had been strangled at or near the airport, Teleford's words were a revelation to me."

Sergeant Wimbling said, "Sounds like Teleford made a few incriminating comments today; you must be good at provocation, Mrs. Huber."

Then he said, "Bill Mc Naught lived in a secluded little shack in walking distance from the Truckee airport. He apparently walked home on Wednesday late afternoon and his killer either followed him, or waited near his home. Two boys bicycling by found the victim a couple of hours later, sprawled out in front of the door, house key in hand."

I saw the dear "leprechaun" clearly in my mind and was filled with sorrow.

The Reno officer looked at Sergeant Wimbling, then at his subordinate. Both gave a barely noticeable nod. He then turned his attention back to me, saying, "Thank you, Mrs. Huber. If we need any further information, we'll contact you. I'm sure you're aware of the fact that sooner or later you'll be called as a witness for the prosecution."

I nodded and got up to leave. At the door I turned around and said, "Officer, I would greatly appreciate being informed of the Lamont & Associates audit results."

He thought about it for a second and then stated, "Once we have them, we might consider sharing them with you."

Chapter 48

By the time I flopped myself onto the hotel room bed at 6 o'clock that evening, I felt totally drained. The day had obviously taken its toll on me. After a few minutes' rest, I called Peter.

He said, "Regula! Are you on your drive down?"

"No, I'm still in Reno. I've decided to stay another night and start for home tomorrow morning."

Perceptive as ever, he asked, "It's all over, isn't it?"

"Yes, Peter – it's over."

"Feel like telling me?"

"With pleasure." And I filled him in on the developments of the case since I had driven into town on Sunday.

Then he said, "I'm stunned! Teleford?" And after a pause he mused, "I figured Bradley was your main suspect!"

"Yes. I suspected Bradley after we came back from Mexico."

"When did you figure out it was Teleford?"

"Not until Friday afternoon when I sat in my office making several calls and kept going over my notes and reviewed in my mind what each and every suspect had revealed to me. I'll explain the whole process to you once I'm home."

Then he commented, "Perdue seems to be a good sport; not everyone would have readily played along with you the way he did. After all, you were a complete stranger to him!"

"Perdue is a great guy!" And I added, "I felt that he liked me too."

"What's there not to like?"

I inquired, "How was your second book-signing day?"

"A big turnout again, just like on Saturday. I'm truly surprised and flattered!"

"Congratulations!"

"Just between you and me, Regula, by late afternoon I thought if I had to smile at one more person and had to scribble one more silly note into a book, I was going to lose my mind!"

"Tell me about the aches and pains of fame!" I teased.

"What are you going to do tonight?"

"I'll have a nice dinner in a quiet place, and then I might turn in. It's been a long day."

Peter exclaimed, "What? You'd resist gambling in a gambling town? I'm shocked!"

"Well, I might get a second wind," I said.

Chapter 49

One day in late May I called Sergeant Wolf.

He said, "Have you figured your retrospect case out yet, Mrs. Huber?"

"It's solved," I replied, "or at least as far as I'm concerned. The Reno and Truckee police officers still have to iron out a few kinks, I'm told."

Then I said, "I'm calling to thank you for your help, Sergeant."

"What did I do?"

"You advised me to go to the head of the firm and request a voluntary audit of their accounts."

He said, "Yes, I remember. So what was the result of the audit he ordered?"

"Oh, he didn't comply, but you set me on the right track by mentioning I should deal with him," I answered.

"I have no idea what you're talking about. You'd better tell me the whole story."

"It's involved. Do you have lots of time?"

He chuckled and said, "Not really, but you've got me interested, so go ahead!"

I stated, "I previously never mentioned any names to you, so I might as well continue my story anonymously." Then I proceeded to tell him the events following our last call, ending with the Reno police's arrest of the murderer and my formal statement at their headquarters.

As I came to a stop, he said, "Well done. Congratulations!"

Then he asked, "Did the Reno Police Department let you in on the result of the audit?"

"Yes," I said. "An officer called and gave me a short version. To tell you the truth, I don't fully understand what was involved. The fraud plotted by the partner was complicated and ingenious. It was a sophisticated Ponzi scheme. The client in Reno had not been the sole victim of the scheme. Numerous others had fallen unsuspecting victims to the fraud. The scam had lasted about a year. The villain had started the swindle five years ago, and it had wound up and stopped just about the time of the plane crash. He had cheated those clients out of enormous sums in the course of that year. My guess is that his plan was to stop the scheme when the new electronic accounting system came into effect, which, by the way, was right around the time the plane crash victim found him out."

The sergeant commented, "Sort of to quit while he was ahead."

"Exactly."

Then he said, "For four years he went undetected. He would have gotten away with the fraud and the murder if it wasn't for that young client of yours finding the note to the lover."

"Yes, I think so. And I added, "But the old mechanic at the Truckee airport would still be alive."

The sergeant sounded perplexed when he asked, "You're not blaming yourself for that fellow's death, I hope?"

"Yes, I guess I am. If I would have thought of asking him the right questions from the beginning, he wouldn't be dead."

"Mrs. Huber! If you let yourself think this way, you're in the wrong line of business!"

He had shocked me with that outburst, but I had to admit his comment was justified.

So I said, "Yes, sir!"

"Sorry to have been so blunt, but I think you needed that."

Then he wanted to know, "Did you find the bug?"

"Not personally, I wouldn't have known what to look for. I hired an expert to tend to the matter after my return from Reno. He didn't have to search far; the device was in the phone receiver."

I heard him laughing out loud and asked, "What's so funny?"

"You're priceless: a detective who doesn't know what a bug looks like!"

"The police officers in Reno seemed to be amused too, but I can't see the humor in it."

After a pause, he said, "Are you working on a new case now?"

"Not at the moment, and I'm thankful for the rest," I remarked.

He said, "I'm looking forward to my rest!"

"Are you planning a vacation soon, Sergeant?"

"No, I was talking about my retirement next March."

"That's less than a year away; the time will fly!"

"I can't wait," he said.

"Do you have any plans once you're retired? I mean any hobbies?"

"I haven't given it a thought yet. I can tell you one thing for sure: It won't have anything to do with crime or criminals!"

"I can understand that."

After a pause, I inquired, "Will I still be able to call on you for advice?"

"Of course!"

"That's good to know."

"Or you can just call for a chat!" he chuckled, and hung up.

EPILOGUE

A month later I was tending to bookkeeping and paying bills at the office. I looked out the window surveying the drab and foggy weather. June gloom seemed to last forever that year. Then the door was pushed open and I faced a couple of visitors.

I exclaimed, "Look who's here! What a pleasant surprise! Come on in."

Michelle Lamont said, "We were in the neighborhood and thought we'd drop by."

I motioned her to the client chair, saying, "Have a seat," and to Scott, "Fetch the folding chair over there," pointing to the far wall.

Then I smiled at the siblings and asked, "Is school out already?"

Scott nodded and said, "Thank God!"

Michelle stated, "I'm staying at Aunt Suzanne and Uncle Keith's before I start my summer classes." And with a wave at Scott, she added, "I'm spending some quality time with my baby brother."

Scott winced at the word "baby," rolling his eyes.

Glancing at the paper work sprawled out all over my desk, Michelle said, "I hope we didn't pick an inconvenient time for our visit?"

"Not at all," I replied, and clearing my desk by shoving everything into the top drawer, I assured her, "There is nothing here that can't wait until later."

Then I pulled out an envelope from the Lamont file, and handing it to Scott, I said, "Your sister paid my fee in full. Here is your deposit back. I had planned to drop it by your house." And I continued, "You can put the money back into your bike fund now!"

He beamed and said, "I've already bought a new mountain bike! It's awesome!"

His sister commented, "He gave it a trial run yesterday. His bike performed so well, I could hardly keep up with him on my old one!"

Then getting serious, she said, "You told us about Thomas Teleford's arrest and what led up to it when you got back from Reno, but there is a lot we don't understand. The police didn't tell us much."

"Police officers can be stingy with giving out information, but we can't really blame them; they have to be careful before a trial."

Scott asked, "But you can tell us, right? You're not under a gag-order or anything?"

I was amused at the boy's choice of vocabulary. He either read crime stories or had tuned-in to media coverage of trials.

I replied, "Not that I'm aware of."

Michelle questioned, "When did you start suspecting Thomas Teleford?"

"Actually, not until late in the game, I'm ashamed to admit."

Scott asked, "Who did you think was the murderer at first?"

"In the beginning," I said, "I suspected everyone."

"Not Michelle and me, though."

"You, Scott, were the only exception. This was a dormant crime that had gone undetected for four years. I could not see any reason you'd have wanted to uncover it, had you been guilty. Therefore, you were the only person I could rule out from the start."

I paused and then asked, "So what do you want to know?"

Without hesitation, Scott said, "Tell it all. I want to know how you found everything out."

"All right. I'll try to explain how I came to my conclusions, step by step. I had to track backward to four years ago. I interviewed all the family members as well as persons connected to the family and your father's business. I didn't know if the motive for the murders was business related or a private matter. The sentence, 'It might make a difference in our relationship,' written in your dad's note to someone named Shelby, tended to point more to a private matter. I felt it was crucial to locate this Shelby and hoped she would be able to throw some light onto the case. When I finally found her, I thought I had made progress."

I continued, "Actually, Shelby Teleford was of no great help to me. She confirmed that she had indeed been Mr. Lamont's girlfriend, but she had no clue as to what the draft letter referred to. In other words, she hadn't any idea what your father planned to investigate when he took off for Los Angeles on the fatal flight. At that point I had interviewed you, Michelle; your Aunt Suzanne and Uncle Keith; your cousins Nicki and Vicki; Thomas Teleford; Teresa Cesar; your father's secretary, Rachael Moreley; and Shelby."

I went on, "I learned a few interesting facts from some of these people, but basically I had not made much progress in my investigation."

Scott questioned, "What facts?"

I smiled, saying, "You really want to know it all, huh? From your sister I learned that she overheard an argument your dad had with someone unknown to her, the evening before his tragic flight. Your dad was apparently angry and had shouted at someone either in person or on the phone.

"Mr. Teleford mentioned that the original plan had been for him to be the passenger on your father's flight, and then this plan had changed at the last minute when your mom took his place instead.

"Rachael Moreley informed me that your father had called her from the Truckee airport before take-off, telling her he would stop by the office. He mentioned that he also wanted to talk with the accountant, James Bradley."

I continued, "Mr. Teleford's remark suggested to me that the murderer might have meant to kill either your father or Mr. Teleford, or both. Rachael Moreley's comment indicated that since your dad wanted to see the accountant, the case might center on a business related matter after all."

I paused and then said, "My next move was to interview the folks at Lake Tahoe. After talking with your Uncle Luke, Aunt Maryanne, and your cousin Chris, I seriously suspected your uncle or possibly your aunt as being the villain for a brief time. There is no reason to dwell on that now, since it proved to be farfetched."

Michelle sent a thankful glance in my direction. I realized at that moment that she either had known or suspected the affair between her mother and Congressman Sosna.

I went on, "Bill Mc Naught told me he had not seen any strangers or anyone suspicious hanging around the airport or the Cessna 152. After coming home from Tahoe, I still felt I was stumbling in the dark where this case was concerned. I hadn't even figured out whether the murderer's motive was business related or of a private matter.

"When you, Michelle, remembered that your dad had talked to a Robert Perdue after skiing at Northstar that day, I was convinced Perdue was the key to the entire mystery.

I was sure that whatever your father had learned from him was crucial in arriving at the core of the matter. I called everybody concerned again, but no one could tell me who Robert Perdue was."

Scott said, "So how did you find him, then?"

"I'll get to that in a moment," I said. And I continued, "As you know, my husband and I ventured on a Central Mexico vacation and combined the trip with a visit to James Bradley, the former accountant of Lamont & Associates. The fact that Bradley had retired just a day after your parents' plane crash could have been a coincidence, but I found it highly suspicious. Bradley proved to be an amiable man in his mid sixties. He gave us an elaborate demonstration on how to grow the most gorgeous orchids. I kept an open mind, however; lots of murderers had been known to show a charming personality!

"Bradley admitted to having seen Robert Perdue's name on paper in his capacity as accountant. This gave the impression that he was innocent, but it could have been a clever way on his part to show he had nothing to hide. Bradley seemed to live in luxury; he owned a plane among other things." And I commented, "By the way, there were far too many people owning private aircrafts in this case, which made it confusing to me. I'll get back to that later."

I continued my chain of thought, "The retired accountant did give me a valuable pointer, though. He remembered that Perdue was a resident of the state of Nevada. I knew now that Perdue had been a client, so I presumed the murderer's motive had to be somehow related to Lamont & Associates. By the time I was sitting on Mexicana Airline on our flight home, James Bradley was my main suspect. I presumed that embezzlement of some kind came into play, and who would've had a better opportunity to carry out such a deed than the accountant?"

Scott said impatiently, "So how come you changed your mind and found out it was Teleford?"

"The day after our return from Mexico I stumbled on the truth, almost by accident. My office had been broken into while out of town. Nothing had been stolen, and I assumed the perpetrator had wanted a look at my Lamont file.

"Amid all the drilling and banging sounding from the door repair crew, I sat at my desk having a major brainstorm! I had made several phone calls earlier, and subconsciously I said to myself: P-e-r-d-u-e, spelling the name out letter by letter. My first call that day had been to a fellow detective in Las Vegas whom I had asked to find a Robert Perdue for me in the state of Nevada. He wanted to know how the name was spelled, and I complied. Then later, I had called Thomas Teleford, and in the course of conversation he also asked me to spell the name. As I spelled out P-e-r-d-u-e once more to Teleford, I thought, déjà vu. Then, during my later brainstorm I contemplated, no, not déjà vu, but rather déjà entendu! Of course, I mused, the reason for the break-in was to plant a listening device in my office."

Scott said, "You mean a bug?"

"Yes, precisely, a bug," I replied.

"And since I was on a Thomas Teleford wave length at the time, I wondered, what if I had the correct motive but the wrong man? Then looking over my notes and searching my mind for what I had learned from each person, I considered all those facts with the idea of Teleford being the criminal. I came to the conclusion that indeed, they all fit with that theory."

Michelle inquired, "And what were those facts?"

I said, "Let's start with Shelby. The excerpt in the note written to her, 'It might make a difference in our relationship,' could have referred to the fact that your dad would expose Shelby's father as a crook. I also remembered that during my talk with Shelby she mentioned that her father had reprimanded her severely for something she wanted explained while working at Lamont & Associates. His words to her were something like, 'Just mind your own business and do the data entry.' I suspected that Shelby had stumbled across something fishy in one of the accounts. I learned from Rachael Moreley that Teleford changed secretaries frequently. That fact also seemed to indicate that he didn't want any of the firm's operations to be watched too closely."

I elaborated further, "No one I had talked to seemed aware that the original plan was for Teleford to be the passenger on your dad's flight to L.A. Teleford could have made this up, and if so, had used this clever move to throw me off. At that point it also occurred to me that if James Bradley remembered the name Robert Perdue, wouldn't it also make sense that Teleford, a partner in the firm, would have come across the client's name as well? So why had he denied it?

"One of my calls earlier that day had been to the Truckee airport. I wanted to ask Bill Mc Naught if he had seen anyone he knew hanging around the airport before Mr. Lamont's take-off. At the time I actually still had Bradley in mind as being the culprit. Even though Bradley did not own his plane yet, he had taken flying instructions just before his retirement. I figured Bill Mc Naught might have known him, but the same was true for Teleford, of course. I happened to know that he had accompanied your father on numerous trips to Truckee, and was known to the mechanic. Obviously, I was too late to ask Mc Naught anything; the old airport mechanic had been strangled two days earlier."

Michelle said, "Poor, funny old Mr. Mc Naught. I liked him a lot. He was a legend at the Truckee airport. I once noticed Dad tipping him, and I asked if it was customary to tip mechanics. I remember Dad's answer clearly. He said, 'Michelle, let me give you a lesson about tipping: The important thing is not whether or not it is customary, but rather whether you appreciate someone's service. Bill Mc Naught has been retired ever since I can remember, and he practically volunteers his time and mechanical skill at this airport. The least I can do is thank him with a tip.'"

Michelle's lips turned up in a melancholic smile as she repeated the words spoken by her father.

I went on, "At that point, Michelle, I also deduced that the confrontation you overheard between your dad and someone was more likely to have been in person and not a phone conversation."

"Why?" she asked.

"I knew that your father did not bring a cell phone or laptop to Tahoe. It was in the evening and after dinner you heard your dad shout the angry words. I doubt he would've had James Bradley's home phone number handy, for instance."

She nodded, and then said, "So the fragment of conversation I overheard that night was my dad yelling at Teleford?"

"No doubt. Your father had summoned his partner to the house that evening and then asked him to step into the den, where he told him the game was up, accusing him of fraud."

"You're right," the young woman said, "the den and my room above it is at the back of the house. I'm sure nobody except me could have overheard them."

I kept going, "So I switched my suspicion to Teleford. When I realized there might be a bug in my office, I thought of all the phone conversations Teleford could have overheard already. Besides the one to my colleague in Vegas, he also heard me talk to a Sergeant Wolf, who suggested I go to the head of the firm asking for a voluntary audit of the files. So when I called Teleford, he was prepared and cunningly agreed to look into the matter. A thing he had no intention of doing, needless to say."

I continued, "I assumed that when he overheard my conversation with the Truckee police, he congratulated himself for having made an impossibility any further questions I might have had for Bill Mc Naught. Even though Teleford's main purpose for breaking into my office was to plant the bug, I was positive he also had scrutinized the Lamont file. He must have understood the significance of the mechanic's statement of not having seen any strangers hanging around. Teleford figured, sooner or later, I would ask Mc Naught if he had seen anyone he knew around the Cessna 152! So he high-tailed it up to Truckee and silenced the old mechanic." And I added, "Whether or not Bill Mc Naught had actually seen Teleford at the airport early that morning, we'll never find out. The fact that the mechanic was strangled seems a strong indication that he did."

I went on, "Coming back to more phone conversations Teleford overheard that day. My contact in Vegas got back to me with the good news of having located Robert Perdue. Subsequently, I called Perdue and scheduled an appointment to see him at 2:00 p.m. the next Monday. I suspected, but couldn't know for sure, that Teleford would try to get up to Reno before me, planning to silence Perdue. So assuming there was a bug planted in my office, I made my second call to Perdue in the parking lot from my cell phone, rescheduling my appointment to Sunday."

With a sigh, I said, "I guess that's all. You already know what happened in Reno."

Scott said, "You were going to tell us something about airplanes."

I laughed and stated, "Nothing escapes you, Scott; I should hire you as my assistant!"

Getting serious again, I said, "So many people involved in the case owned planes that it made matters more complicated for me. Actually, it turned out those aircrafts were of no importance at all."

He stared and then said, "What do you mean?"

I explained, "I didn't word that well. What I meant is, besides your father, also your Uncle Luke, Thomas Teleford and James Bradley owned planes. In the beginning I thought it might be important to know exactly what kind of machines each one of them owned, but as I said, this proved insignificant.

"In the early stages of my investigation when I suspected everyone, I deduced that it would've been possible for the individuals not present at Lake Tahoe to take a night flight to Reno, drive to the Truckee airport by rental car or cab, do the dirty deed to the Cessna 152 and take an early morning flight back to L.A."

Scott interrupted, "What individuals?"

"Rachael Moreley or James Bradley, and yes, I even considered Shelby. I felt it was safe to exclude Teresa Cesar, since she was in Panama at the time."

I went on, "Then, for instance, when I found out my office had been broken into on Tuesday night, I immediately jumped to the wrong conclusion. At the time I suspected Bradley as being the guilty party, so I calculated if it would have been possible, time-wise, for him to fly here after I had seen him in Central Mexico that Monday afternoon. And again, after I heard the news that Mr. Mc Naught had been strangled on Wednesday afternoon, I was assuming a plane had been the way of transportation. I knew the killer would not dare to actually fly into Truckee, but I was going to check with the airports at South Tahoe and Reno for data.

"Then suddenly I realized how stupid I'd been. No one on his way to commit murder would risk flying into any airport in the area, whether in a private plane or by commercial flight. So obviously that meant the killer had to have driven up."

After a pause, Michelle asked, "How did Teleford manage to embezzle money from the firm?"

"Actually, he stole from numerous clients," I stated. "Perdue wasn't the only one."

"How?"

"I don't understand the details, but he cleverly plotted a sophisticated Ponzi scheme to defraud the clients he chose. He apparently hand-picked the clients, most of them residing out of State."

Scott said, "What's a Ponzi scheme?"

Before I could think up an explanation, Michelle answered him, saying, "It's a scheme where one borrows from Peter to pay Paul."

"That's a good comparison," I said, "but Teleford's scam was much more complicated than the average Ponzi scheme."

"Why?" Scott asked.

"Why was it complicated?"

"No, I mean why did he do it? I'm sure he wasn't poor."

"Greed. Simply greed," I stated.

I paused, and then continued, "James Bradley was involved."

Michelle exclaimed, "Really?"

"On the long drive to Reno I mulled over the case and wondered how a long-time accountant at the firm could have been oblivious to Teleford's fraudulent actions for an entire year. He must have at least suspected something, I determined. Had Bradley possibly been involved in the scam? Later, I mentioned my concern about the accountant to the Reno police in my statement."

Michelle questioned, "And was Bradley really an accomplice?"

"He was innocent of anything that had to do with the killings, but he knew about Teleford's swindle."

"How so?"

I explained, "Bradley did get wise to the scheme and questioned Teleford about it. At the time it was an established fact that the bookkeeper wanted to retire when the new accounting system came into effect. So Teleford made a bargain with Bradley to say nothing and use his talents to run a 'double' set of books. The fake set would be presented to the outside auditors so that they could not uncover the scam. In exchange for his silence and cooperation, Teleford paid Bradley off. The accountant could not resist the temptation. The extra money would come in handy for his retirement. Bradley felt the deal would go undetected, as he'd be heading for Mexico. And since the plan was to end the fraud with the installation of the new accounting system, it would be almost impossible to 'backtrack' as long as no one raised a warning flag."

Michelle asked, "So nothing happens to Bradley?"

I declared, "Even though he is innocent of the murders, he will be extradited and brought back to the U.S. as a witness to testify at the Teleford trial, possibly in exchange for a lenient sentence relative to his role in the fraud scheme."

Then Scott wanted to know, "What did Teleford do to Dad's Cessna?"

"I'm pretty sure he sabotaged the plane by contaminating the fuel. I doubt this can be proven after so many years, however," I said, regretfully.

Then Michelle questioned, "How did Dad know Teleford was the crook after he talked to Perdue? The swindle could just as well have been orchestrated by Bradley or one of the junior brokers."

"Good point, Michelle!" I said. "The thought had crossed my mind too. Either something in the statement sent to Perdue identified it as being Teleford's account, or, more likely, your father had suspected his partner of fraudulent activities prior to that day. He might have kept an eye on Teleford, and the 'Perdue discovery' would have been the last straw."

She commented, "So from Teleford's point of view, he thought that he had gotten away with the swindle, and suddenly Dad was about to blow the whistle and ruin everything! Therefore, he resorted to sabotaging the plane."

"Precisely."

After a pause Michelle remarked, "I feel sorry for Shelby Teleford."

I nodded. "She'll have to cope with the knowledge that her father murdered the person she loved." And I added, "She's getting married soon, which might help."

Scott stated, "I don't feel sorry for her; she had no business being Dad's girlfriend."

Michelle patted her brother's shoulder and said, "Let's put all this behind us now, Scott."

We sat in silence for some time, and then I turned to the young woman, saying, "By any chance, do you have any errands to run in Pasadena? I'd like to be left alone with Scott for a while."

She stared at me perplexed. Then she smiled, and remarked, "I wonder what secrets you two could possibly have?" And getting to her feet, she announced, "I'm always looking for a good excuse to head for the mall!"

As soon as the door shut behind her, I said, "All right, Scott, let's get down to business. I challenge you to a chess rematch."

I had improved my game considerably.
This time it took the boy at least 100 moves to beat me!

Printed in the United States
37245LVS00003B/1-15